NEWS AND NECTARINES

A SMALL TOWN COZY MYSTERY

CARLY WINTER

Edited by
DIVAS AT WORK EDITING
Cover Design
COVERSBYMELINDA.COM

WESTWARD PUBLISHING

Cover Design by CoversByMelinda.com

NEWS AND NECTARINES

She's trying to report on the facts, but someone is framing her for murder.

A local nectarine orchard burning to the ground is front-page news, and as the only reporter for the Tri-Town Times, Tilly Donner is determined to uncover the facts and find out who started the fire. That is, until she finds the main suspect with a knife in his chest, taking his dying breaths.

With the help of her two best friends and the local small-town gossip vine, Tilly uncovers clues to help the police solve the case. But her plan backfires when the Sheriff believes the evidence leads to Tilly being the killer.

Can Tilly discover who committed the murder and prove her innocence before her reputation and life are ruined?

1

Boom. Whoosh. Boom.

Three things happened when I thought the end of the world had arrived at one o'clock in the morning.

First, I sat up in bed as terror ripped through me.

Second, so did my dog, a Golden Retriever named Tinker.

Third, while I tried to get out of bed, Tinker attempted to crawl *under* the covers and caused my legs to get tied up in the sheet, which led to me hitting my head on the nightstand as I fell to the floor headfirst and landed with a loud *thump*.

"Ow!" I yelled, grabbing my forehead.

My black cat, Belle, barely gave me a second glance as she tore out of the room.

I was finally able to free myself from the clutches of my sheets and stagger to my feet, then to the window.

My small town of Oak Peak wasn't under attack, nor had aliens invaded. Instead, fireworks went off in Mr. York's yard and had apparently caught my other neighbors'—the Ruperts—nectarine orchard on fire. The trees resembled dancing demons when flames shot up into the air.

As I ran to my closet with nothing but the fire outside illuminating my room, I stubbed my toe on my bed frame and hit my shoulder on the closet door. I winced and cursed, then pulled off my nightgown and threw it to the floor. I found a sweatshirt and some jeans I had worn the previous day, then quickly dressed. Just as I pulled on my rain boots, I heard Tinker throw up.

"Tinker!" I yelled as I stumbled toward the light switch, which I quickly realized was the first thing I should have done. When the room illuminated, I found Tinker standing on my bed retching her guts out all over my blue and yellow comforter.

After screaming at her again, which only seemed to make the vomiting worse, I took a brief moment to decide what was more important: the dog barfing on my bed, or the flames in the nectarine orchard?

And, were my animals safer inside the house, or did I try to herd them out?

I turned and ran into the hallway, then down the stairs, hoping Belle wouldn't trip me up. I didn't think I could take too many more injuries in such a short period of time. A lump had already begun to form on my forehead just above my right eye and my toe throbbed in my boot.

As I skidded to a stop outside my front door, I tried to figure out which way to go while my heart thundered in my chest. The flames consumed the trees but didn't seem to be creeping any closer to my property. The fireworks had come from my other neighbor, Mr. York. Since I couldn't get to the Ruperts' house, I decided to head over to see Mr. York.

"Tinker! Belly-Belle!" I yelled. "Come on! Let's go out!"

When neither appeared, I once again gauged the distance of the fire and decided they'd be safe in the house. If I actually got them outside, I'd probably never see Belle again and Tinker would be an even bigger wreck than she already was. Deciding to keep a close eye on the fire, I'd come home if I felt my house was in danger.

Sirens wailed in the distance while a few more

fireworks lit up the night sky. I sprinted across the two acres separating my house from Mr. York's. After climbing through the fence, I found him in the back of his property, hose in hand, trying to spray down the railing and shed that had caught fire.

"Mr. York!"

He turned to me and then centered his attention back to the flames.

"What happened?" I asked when I stood next to him. Barely able to breathe, I placed my hands on my knees. Man, was I out of shape.

"Looks like the fireworks in my shed went off and started a fire," he replied.

"Why in the world did you have fireworks?"

We both glanced over our shoulders as a firetruck raced into my property and firemen began unraveling hoses and motioning us back toward Mr. York's home.

From this angle, I could see my property wouldn't be in any danger. The fire had at least a half-acre before it arrived at my door and the firemen had set up between my house and the orchard.

Glancing up, I saw Tinker's silhouette in the bedroom window as she stood on her hind legs and placed her paws on the windowsill. A moment later she disappeared and I prayed her stomach had calmed down a little bit. She always became sick when stressed or upset. Hopefully, the runs wouldn't kick in as well because that would be one heck of a mess.

"Why do you have fireworks?" I asked again as we strode toward his house. I had to take two steps for every one of his since we were complete opposites. He stood tall and thin, and I was short and... let's just say there was more of me to love than there had been when I first moved into town.

We took a seat on his swing chair on his side deck and watched the show.

"Are you here asking as my neighbor and friend, or as a reporter?"

I placed Mr. York in his sixties. As a widower, he lived alone and had once owned the property my house was built on, as well as the orchard and the house directly behind him. The land had been chopped up into four squares and he'd secured his retirement by selling. Well, that's what I'd heard through the gossip vine.

"As your friend," I said firmly as I tucked a lock of my blonde hair behind my ear.

I was the lone reporter for the Tri-Town Times, and sometimes people didn't like to talk to me.

"They aren't mine," he said, scratching his balding head. "I was keeping them for someone."

"But they've been illegal for twenty years!"

"Actually, twenty-two."

"Really?"

"Yes."

"Time sure goes by fast," I said shaking my head.

"What are you, Tilly? Thirty? Thirty-five? Wait until you get to my age. You won't believe how quickly the days fly by."

Actually, thirty-seven, but I didn't bother to correct him.

I had arrived at the time of my life where it had become obvious that I was no longer in my twenties. Little lines had appeared around my eyes. My complexion seemed a bit drab. I needed more mois-turizer and I worried about sunscreen. I rarely got carded anymore if I bought booze, and sometimes it made me a little sad. My youth seemed to be fading with each passing day as I began my trek into middle age.

And when I thought about it all, I became angry. Stupid ex-husband had ruined all our plans.

Based on the firemen's easygoing banter and their relaxed stances as they worked the hoses, it became apparent the flames would be out in a short while.

Fireworks had been banned twenty-two years ago by the current Mayor Shelton's father when he'd served in the same position. I hadn't lived in town then, but apparently during a Fourth of July celebration, the whole dang main drag had burned to the ground with nothing left but piles of ashes. And from what I had heard, I mean *everything*. From one end of Oak Avenue to the other had been eaten by the fire. The bank, the pharmacy, the grocery store—every building.

Northern California tended to be drought prone, and that year had been particularly bad. The mayor and city council at that time had passed laws banning fireworks, both big and small, and initiated heavy fines if the laws were broken. As I'd been told, not one single townsperson bothered to oppose them. In fact, they stopped celebrating the holiday altogether. To the folks of Oak Peak, the Fourth of July was just another hot, summer day.

"Who had you hold them?" I asked.

Mr. York arched an eyebrow at me and crossed his arms over his chest.

"Off the record," I muttered. "I'm here as a neighbor and friend, remember?"

His wrinkles deepened around his blue eyes as he grinned. "This is just between you and me, okay?"

"Of course."

He glanced around as if checking to make sure no one eavesdropped on us, which seemed a little ridiculous to me. We had at least an acre separating us from the firefighters, and more spanned to our neighbors' houses. Not to mention the fire.

"The mayor."

I'd never really been good at hiding my emotions, and I gasped as my mouth fell open in surprise.

"Mayor Shelton?" I shrieked.

"Shh, Tilly," Mr. York chastised as he brought his index finger to his mouth. "Someone will hear you."

I glanced around, unsure who that would be, but let the statement lie. If Mr. York wasn't comfortable talking about it, I'd lower my voice.

We sat in silence for a moment as I processed the secret. "Why would he even want fireworks around here?"

"Well, since his dad passed last year, he's been thinking about bringing back the Fourth of July cele-bration. Big fireworks, hand-held fireworks, town picnic... the whole shebang."

I chewed my bottom lip as I considered the plan.

"Fourth of July is next month. Is that a showing of outright disrespect, or is the mayor trying to prove himself to the people of Oak Peak?"

There had been rumors the mayor didn't have many allies in town, but I really didn't know much. The city council may not like him, but they kept their mouths shut when I was around.

Mr. York shrugged. "I don't know. He asked me to help him out, so I did. His dad and I were good friends. I didn't ask any questions."

"Who lit them?" I asked. "You didn't, did you?"

"No," he replied as he shook his head. "I didn't. I don't know who did, though."

As smoke filled the air and the flames died down at the back of the orchard, I could see the red and white fire truck lights at the front of it, and I hoped the Ruperts' home hadn't been burnt.

I couldn't help but feel like Mr. York was lying to me and he knew exactly who had lit them.

"Can fireworks spontaneously... combust? Or whatever?"

"Not that I know of."

"Well, if you didn't light them, who did?"

Mr. York chuckled. "I don't know, Tilly. I think that's something for the police to discover."

Five minutes later, a sheriff's cruiser pulled into

Mr. York's driveway. I groaned when the driver sauntered up to us.

"What happened here?" Deputy Byron Mills
asked.

"Looks like there was a little accident," Mr. York
said, and I giggled at his sarcasm.

I had dated Byron briefly after my husband left
me. After three dinners, brawny and brainless was
my opinion of him. Brown hair, brown eyes, and a
physique that belonged on the cover of a romance
novel, but he didn't do much for me.

However, he didn't seem to get the message that I
wasn't interested. The best course of action would
have been for me to say it outright, but I wasn't good
at confrontation and saying my piece. Instead, I
ignored his calls, crossed the street when I saw him
coming, and hurried down another aisle in the
grocery store before he could say hello.

"Aren't you going to say hi, Tilly?" Byron asked.

"Hi, Byron."

"It's nice to see you again, Tilly. I've called you a
couple of times. It always goes to voicemail."

"Really?" I replied, furrowing my brow as if
trying to recall the twenty voicemails he'd left in the
past month. "I'm sorry about that. I've been really
busy."

That seemed to appease him as he took his concentration from me to the fire.

"I thought I saw fireworks out this way from town," he said.

"That's because you did," Mr. York replied. "And that's what started the fire."

"Who had them?" Byron asked as he pulled out a small notepad from his back pocket. "Who lit them? They're going to get some hefty fines. Maybe jail."

I pursed my lips together and stared at the firemen. It wasn't my place to answer the question.

"They were on my property," Mr. York replied. "But I didn't light them."

"Why did you have fireworks?" Byron asked.

With a sigh, I stood. "I'm heading back to my house. My dog threw up on my bed before I left and I need to get it cleaned up."

"Goodnight, Tilly," the two men said in unison, and I waved at them over my shoulder.

When I returned to the house, the scent of dog poo assaulted me. Apparently, Tinker had become very upset.

"Tinker! Belle!" I yelled.

Belle came around the corner and meowed loudly, then stalked off into the living room. Tinker slinked down the stairs with her tail tucked between her legs.

"It's okay," I said as I scratched behind her ears. "I know you didn't mean to. Let's get it cleaned up. Who's my good girl?'"

The dog wagged her tail and finally met my gaze.

I grabbed some paper towels and carpet cleaner from the kitchen, then went upstairs, the smells getting stronger. As I surveyed the damage to my comforter and the area rug in my room, I knew I would be in for a long night of cleaning.

While pulling the sheets from my bed, I couldn't help but wonder who had lit the fireworks, and why.

It was definitely a mystery, but I'd leave the sleuthing to the police.

2

MY ALARM DIDN'T WAKE me the next morning—Tinker did with her barking as she ran down the stairs.

With a groan, I rolled over and saw that my alarm had been set to go off in ten minutes. The cleanup from last night had taken far longer than I anticipated, and those extra ten minutes would have been nice.

Tinker continued barking and I finally heard someone knocking on my front door. They obviously weren't going away and Tinker wasn't going to shut up... so my day had begun.

I pulled on my robe and headed downstairs.

"I'm coming!" I yelled as another knock sounded, hoping I didn't sound too angry, when really, I'd have liked nothing more than to give the person who had stolen those precious ten minutes from me a piece of my mind. However, I'd been raised in the heartland and down south, and mama made sure I knew not to be rude, even when I wanted to be.

My neighbor, Minnie Johnson, stood on my porch.

"Hi, Tilly," she said. "I was wondering if you'd seen my cows, but I can see you just rolled out of bed."

"You're right," I replied with a yawn. "I haven't seen them."

Minnie was a few years older than me, twice divorced and had a son who was away at college. We weren't exactly friends because I had absolutely nothing in common with her, but we were neighborly. She wanted to always do things like hike, take a bike ride, or do pull-ups in the barn, and I preferred to read in my spare time. That's why she had the body of a super model and I resembled a marshmallow.

"What's that smell?" she asked, crinkling her nose. "Did Tinker have an accident?"

"You can still smell it?"

"Oh, yes."

"Darn it," I said with a sigh. "I was up for hours cleaning the mess last night."

"Did Tinker get scared?"

"Yes. She threw up and pooped all over my bedroom from the fireworks."

"That was something else, wasn't it?" Minnie asked. "That's when the cows got loose. The fireworks scared them to death and they busted right through the fence."

I simply nodded because the truth was, Minnie's cows, Tulip and Sunflower, were always loose. She could usually find them eating the nectarines in the Ruperts' yard, but cows would run from the fire, not to it.

"I'd better get going," Minnie said with a wave. "I've got to find them before they hurt themselves."

Most people in our area raised cattle for the milk or the meat. Minnie had bought Tulip and Sunflower after her son went to college, with the idea she'd sell them off to slaughter. Instead, she'd fallen in love with both of them and I'd never seen cows who had it so good. She showered them with attention, kept their stalls spotless, and spoiled them rotten with lots of fruits and vegetables. Sometimes I thought they ate better than I did.

Upstairs, my alarm began blaring, and I sighed,

wondering how I was going to make it through the day. A lot of coffee would certainly be in order.

I hurried up the stairs and turned off the alarm, then undressed and got into the shower, realizing I was completely out of shampoo. I'd been scraping the bottle for a good week and had meant to stop by the store on my way home from work the prior day, but I'd forgotten.

After a quick wash, I stepped from the shower to find Belle eyeing me critically, her tail swishing back and forth.

"Don't judge me," I muttered as I dried off. "I'll lose the weight eventually."

Trying to ignore the silent critic, I turned to the mirror. I stood about five foot two. When I had moved to Oak Peak, I had been a size four. Now, I was a tight size twelve. I'd gained most of the weight over the past year after my husband had left me, and it was then I realized I was an emotional eater. One day soon I'd start watching what I ate, and maybe even join Minnie in the barn for some pull-ups.

Well, probably not the latter, but I'd lose what I'd gained.

Deep purple circles hung under my eyes and I immediately knew no amount of concealer would get rid of them. My hair would be a greasy mess since I didn't have any shampoo, and the lump on my forehead had turned a light shade of blue that matched my eyes. It wouldn't be one of my better days. I glanced down at the toe I'd stubbed the previous night to find it swollen and an ugly shade of violet.

Good thing it was summer and I could wear sandals.

After quickly dressing, I went downstairs with Belle at my feet. I let Tinker out, who immediately raced around the yard and sniffed at the back fence where the fire had been. When I opened the cabinet where I kept the cat food, my stomach sank. Not only did I need shampoo, but cat food as well.

I glanced down at Belle, who now meowed as well as cast her judgmental glare upon me.

"Belly-Belle, I don't have any food for you."

The cat gave me a piece of her mind, then stalked off.

"I'm not going to leave you hungry!" I called. "Do you want some tuna?"

Checking for the tuna before offering it would have been a good idea. Thankfully, I did find a can, and I placed the contents in her bowl. She didn't come scampering back, and I figured I'd hurt her feelings by forgetting her food. She'd probably leave a hairball on my pillow for the slight.

"I'll get some tonight, I promise!"

After laying down Tinker's breakfast, I called her inside the house. I was happy to see her running with her tongue lolling to the side like last night never happened.

I pulled the sheets from the washer and threw them in the dryer, then opened a few windows in hopes the house would air out. The summer day held a bit of a breeze, but I'd take the smell of charred nectarine trees over dog poo anytime. I also unlatched Tinker's dog door. I kept it closed at night because one morning I found a raccoon in the kitchen after my ex-husband, Tommy, had already left for work. I'd slipped on the rug by the sink and broke my arm while trying shoo the angry coon out the door, and I often wondered if Tommy had seen it, but decided to let me handle it. I mean, how do you miss a raccoon sitting on the counter eating the banana bread I'd baked the previous night? And that little guy wouldn't give it up, either. After I fell, I ended up chucking the whole loaf out the door, and the little thief followed.

"I'm leaving! I'll miss you two! Be good!"

Did other people talk to their pets as much as I

did, or was I destined to be the old spinster who spoke to no one but them?

With a sigh, I slid into my blue pickup truck and headed toward town. On a whim, I turned into Mr. York's driveway just to see what Byron had said to him after I left. I had plenty of time before I had to be at work.

As I cut the ignition, I glanced around the property for him. The charred orchard looked like the forest of evil and death, the black twisted and gnarled branches bouncing in the breeze. Mr. York's back fence had been burnt just a bit and the shed was nothing but a skeleton, but other than that, everything looked normal.

Still, I couldn't shake the feeling something was very wrong.

I got out of the truck and knocked on his front door. I was surprised to see it swing open and a chill of fear sped down my spine.

"Mr. York?" I yelled, telling myself all the reasons his front door would have been ajar.

Maybe he'd been outside and had to use the bathroom, then ran back into the house and hadn't properly shut the door.

Or, he'd had an early morning visitor and they sat in the kitchen right now having coffee and donuts. Mr. York hadn't realized the door hadn't shut.

These possibilities calmed me down and I called for him again. No answer.

I peeked my head in and saw the stairs leading to the second floor and the hallway to the kitchen. The silence became deafening as I decided what to do.

Instead of barging into his house, I walked around to the garage to see if his car was there. I glanced into the window and spotted the old white Chevy. He didn't have another vehicle, so he had to be home—unless someone came and picked him up, but I also knew he didn't socialize much.

I walked around the other side of the house to make sure he wasn't in the back area. I felt a lot more comfortable doing that than going into his home uninvited.

As I meandered around the house, I hummed a Back Street Boys tune. The noise became my companion and calmed my nerves.

"Mr. York!" I called again, the bad feeling spreading in my gut.

Where had he gone?

When I had circled the whole house, I studied the yard once again. The grass had grown really tall by the back fence and shed where the fire had been.

I once again debated whether I should go into the house. He could have fallen and not been able to help himself. If that were the case, I couldn't leave him all day because I was nervous about invading his privacy.

I walked toward the shed to check out the damage while trying to work up the courage to go into the house. My hesitation seemed ridiculous, but I didn't want to catch him naked. That would make our relationship very uncomfortable. Childish, I know.

As I shuffled through the tall grass, I hoped there weren't any snakes that had decided to lie out in the summer sun. I really hated the creatures.

I almost tripped over Mr. York. He lay prone in the grass with his eyes closed. A knife with a decorative red and blue hilt stuck out of his chest. I gasped while falling to my knees and checked for a pulse. It was weak, but his ribs still moved up and down slowly.

"Mr. York!" I yelled, unsure of what to do. "What happened?"

Well, he'd been stabbed. That was pretty obvious.

"Who did this?"

He didn't answer but his eyes fluttered open.

"I need to call an ambulance!" I said as I tried to stagger to my feet. I'd left my phone in the car.

He grabbed my hand and held me in place.

"I-I know... "

His words came out in a whisper.

"What? You know what?"

"I... I... know who lit them."

"The fireworks? You know who lit the fireworks?"

In my panic, I realized I was yelling at him.

"They did this."

So the person who had buried a knife in his chest and the person who had lit the fireworks were the same individual?

He lifted his hand from the grass and pointed toward the sky.

"Who?" I asked, glancing upward. "God? The clouds? Birds?"

He shut his eyes and his breathing became even more labored.

I got to my feet and ran to my truck, then dialed 9-1-1 with shaky hands. Once I gave them the address, I hurried back to Mr. York.

His chest had completely stilled and I touched his shoulder while tears cascaded down my cheeks.

"Don't die, Mr. York," I whispered, and then I realized I didn't even know his first name. How odd.

We'd been neighbors for two years, and I'd always called him Mr. York.

The ambulance arrived moments later. I stood and waved them over. They drove right through the grass to us.

Two paramedics, a man and a woman, jumped out and I moved to the side. I knew what they were going to say.

After a brief examination, the two looked at each other, then shook their heads.

The woman got to her feet and turned to me. "I'm sorry, hon, but he's passed."

I nodded as the other medic got on the radio to call it in.

"Did you know him?" the woman asked me.

I nodded as tears streamed down my face. I couldn't take my gaze away from Mr. York.

"Did you find him like this?"

"Yes."

"Do you know who would want to do this to him?"

I glanced at the sky, trying to understand why he'd pointed upward. "No."

"The police will be here soon," she said, resting her hand on my forearm. "Can you wait and give your statement?"

"Yes."

As they loaded his body into the ambulance, I shuffled to the front porch and sat down on the swing we'd shared the prior night.

Mr. York said the person who had lit the fireworks and the one had killed him were the same person.

But who? I stared at the blue summer sky. A few wispy clouds floated by, and I had a hard time reconciling the peaceful sight with the horror of finding Mr. York.

A fire. A death. And one person responsible. The police definitely had their hands full.

3

As I DROVE the two-lane highway through the forest into town, I swiped at the tears that didn't seem to want to stop.

My statement to the police had consisted of me bawling my eyes out and Byron attempting to comfort me. He'd tried to ask me a few questions, but I couldn't talk beyond all the snot clogging my throat. When he'd attempted to put his arm around me, it only made me sob even worse. Finally, he gave up and said he'd be by to get my statement the next day.

I hadn't bothered letting my boss, Harold, know that I would be late. He used to work as an editor of the LA Times but retired to Oak Peak where he quickly grew bored and opened his own paper. He did the ad sales, editing, and printing, while I wrote the articles. The paper came out twice a month as not much happened int the Tri-Towns, and Harold never ceased to complain about it. I swear, if he could manufacture news for his paper, he would.

Tri-Towns consisted of three towns in the form of a triangle, all about thirty miles away from each other. Oak Peak made up the bottom right, Cedarville the bottom left, and Little River sat at the top. All together, the population was about ten thousand.

When I pulled up in front of The Tri-Town Times paper's premises, I turned off the ignition and stared out the front window. Located on the main drag, Oak Avenue, it sat next to the florist, Sunny Creations, and Debbie's Deliciousness, the bakery, was two doors down.

My mouth watered at the thought of a crème-filled donut and a coffee. The sadness and stress of my morning overwhelmed me, and I realized I was about to dive headfirst into emotional eating. I squeezed the steering wheel with both hands while debating whether the donut would be worth it.

Yes. Yes, it would.

If watching my neighbor die didn't deserve a

little donut to help ease the pain, I don't know what did.

I jumped from my truck and hurried down the street, determined not to change my mind.

Debbie stood behind the case writing on a pad of paper. A few years older than me, she wore her hair flaming red and cut in a pixie style. Her green eyes always danced with happiness and mischief, and she never hid the fact she loved to gossip. Some people chattered all day long, but then acted offended when called out. Debbie just grinned and shrugged her shoulders. I really liked that she owned up to it, and honestly, she was my best source in town, as well as one of my best friends. Debbie knew everyone and everything about everyone. I appreciated her knack of getting people to talk to her and also her friendship.

She'd never married or had kids, and we joked we'd grow to be the old spinsters in town living together and yelling at kids to get off our lawn while we imbibed in our lunchtime cocktails.

Her smile turned into a frown as she studied me and walked around the counter. "Matilda Elizabeth Donner. What in the world happened to you?"

Debbie took me into a big bear hug and I closed

my eyes to hold back the tears. I had to admit, the human touch felt nice.

"My neighbor, Mr. York, was murdered."

She gasped and held me at arm's length. "Oh, my goodness, Tilly. Tell me what happened. Do you want some coffee?"

"Yes. And a crème donut."

She pulled out a chair and pointed at it, then hurried back around the counter as I sat down. She returned with two coffees and my comfort food.

We sat in silence as I inhaled my donut. Sadly, I didn't feel any different after picking every last crumb from my plate.

"What happened to your head?" she asked.

I gently touched my fingertips to the knot above my eyebrow. "That was from last night. I fell out of bed and hit my head on the nightstand. There was a fire in my neighbors' yard."

"I heard about that. But I thought it happened in the Ruperts' nectarine orchard?"

"Yes," I said with a nod. "It did." It didn't surprise me she knew about the fire. The gossip vine had most likely come alive pretty early this morning when the fire department and the cops all went home and told their loved ones about their night.

"So you had a fire in one neighbor's yard last

night, then Henry York was murdered this morning?"

I stared at her a beat before speaking. "I didn't know his name was Henry. I just always called him Mr. York."

"Oh, honey," Debbie said as she reached across the table and took my hand. "It's okay. He was old school like that. He probably appreciated the respect you showed him."

A tear escaped and tracked down my cheek. I quickly wiped it away.

"Such a sad state of affairs," Debbie said, shaking her head. "Do they know who did it?"

"Probably not. The police just started their investigation."

"What do you think happened?"

Debbie fished for information, but I really didn't have any to give her. "I don't know," I replied with a shrug. "Mr. York said the person who killed him was the same person who lit the fireworks."

"Fireworks?!" Debbie screeched. "I didn't know about that!"

I told her the story of the fireworks starting the fire, and how Mr. York had been holding them for the mayor.

"What a conniving little turd that mayor is,"

Debbie muttered. "He was a young boy when the town burnt down and probably doesn't remember the devastation. I was in my early twenties and recall it well. Just as his daddy had said when he'd banned them, fireworks don't belong here."

I finished my coffee and got to my feet. "I'm late for work."

Debbie stood and grabbed my plate and empty cup. "Don't worry about this. It's on the house, hon. You've had a rough day, and if one of my donuts can make you feel a little better, then I'm happy to feed it to you."

"Thank you."

I did feel better, but I wondered if it was from the donut or Debbie's company.

As I walked to the door, I had an interesting thought. I usually tried to stay out of gossip, but there was a murderer running around town, and he or she had struck very close to my home.

I turned to Debbie. "If you hear anything, will you call me?"

A sly grin spread over her face. "Of course, Tilly. You do the same."

I nodded and headed two doors down to the paper. Harold eyed me over his glasses from his desk as I walked in.

"Where have you been, Tilly? I must have called six times."

I flopped down into my chair and sighed. It was only ten in the morning and I was exhausted. "I was up all night dealing with the fire and cleaning dog vomit and poo. Tinker got scared from the fireworks. Then my neighbor, Mr. York, was murdered this morning."

"Murdered?!" Harold said, shooting to his feet. "Did you interview the police?"

"No. I found the body and I was too upset to give the—"

"You found the body?" Harold asked excitedly as he paced our small office.

"Yes."

"This is gold, Tilly. Absolute gold."

I furrowed my brow at his obvious giddiness. "Harold, someone died. His corpse probably isn't even cold yet. Have a little respect."

My eyes welled once again and I glanced at the mess on my desk to hide them from my boss. He may have been some hard-nosed, big-city editor bothered by nothing, but I wasn't that way. Mr. York's death and finding the body had hit me pretty hard.

Silence blanketed the office for a few moments as I fought back my tears. I hadn't cried this much in my life, even when my father had died or when my husband left me.

"I'm sorry," Harold finally said. "I'd heard about the fireworks, but not the murder. I got a little ahead of myself there. Were you two really friendly?"

"A bit," I said with a shrug. "He was a nice man."

I heard the creak of Harold's chair when he sat down. "Do you want me to write the story? Are you too close to it?"

"No," I said with a sigh. "Well, maybe about Mr. York's murder. I don't know. I'm just so exhausted right now, everything seems like too much. I don't think I could get out of this chair if I tried."

"Okay," Harold said with a nod. "Then let's just talk things out, if that's all right with you."

"Sure," I replied, stretching my arms over my head. "Go ahead."

"I see a sequence of stories here. First, the fireworks you mentioned. Where were they? How did they get lit? Who brought them into town?"

"The mayor."

Harold arched an eyebrow. "Okay, well... that right there is one hell of a story. We're going to have to interview him. How did you discover it was the mayor?"

"Mr. York told me last night. It was supposed to

be a secret, but he's dead now. It's important."

I pulled out a pad of paper and made a note: *Interview mayor about fireworks.*

"Then we have the human side of the story," Harold continued. "Who was affected by the fire? How?"

Interview Ruperts and Minnie for humanity piece.

"And of course, the murder. We can get a few stories out of that. An article about the victim. Police interviews. Once they catch the killer, coverage of the trial. When was the last time someone was murdered around here anyhow?"

"I don't know," I replied with a shrug as I jotted it down. "I've been here almost three years and can't recall anyone being killed."

"I've been in Oak Peak going on eight years and I can verify there hasn't been a murder. That right there is news in itself."

"The town's going to be in an uproar. Everything going to heck in a handbasket and all that."

"You're exactly right."

We stared at each other a beat and the sinking feeling of being overwhelmed came over me. He was right. A lot of reporting lay ahead.

Not a lot happened in our small part of the world. The columns I usually wrote were about bake sales to benefit the high school teams, a feature on a new business that had moved into the Tri-Towns, or what happened at the city council meeting. Now, I was moving into really heavy-hitting stuff like illegal activity by the mayor and a murder. My stomach twisted and I began to feel a little sick.

"Okay, here's what we're going to do," Harold said, getting to his feet. "You take today off. I can see you're beat up both literally and figuratively. What happened to your head?"

"Fell out of bed once the fireworks started going off last night."

"You might want to have that checked out. I'm worried you might have a concussion. That knot is turning a really awful shade of purple."

"Thanks," I muttered as I rolled my eyes.

"So, anyway, you go home. Relax. Get some sleep. Think about seeing the doctor. Tomorrow you hit it hard. I want at least one humanity piece on my desk by five at the latest. We can put out a special edition on Thursday. The whole town will be talking about it, so copies will go fast. I better start calling around for advertising. Everyone's going to be looking at this paper, and it's a great opportunity for the businesses of the Tri-Town area to be seen."

I realized he wasn't really talking to me anymore,

but more to himself. And he was right about everything. I felt completely useless and drained. A day at home snuggled with Tinker and Belle watching soap operas and eating ice cream sounded like the perfect cure.

And this story was the biggest thing to hit our area since the dairy farm over in Cedarville closed about a year ago.

The whole town would be gossiping within the next few hours when Debbie started chatting with anyone who went into her bakery, and come tomorrow, I'd have a lot of half-truths and lies to wade through while I interviewed people and wrote my stories.

Frankly, unlike Harold, I preferred the quiet serenity our small town offered. I liked that I could sleep with my windows open without giving it a second thought, or leave my truck running on Oak Avenue while I ran into the pharmacy to pick up a prescription. I certainly didn't like the queasy feeling this murder had given me, the way I felt I had to look over my shoulder for fear of being next.

Way too close to home...

Hopefully, the police would solve the crime quickly and we could once again enjoy our sleepy little town.

4

I WOKE the next morning feeling refreshed and
more like myself. My plan of cuddling with my fur
babies and watching soap operas all day had come
to fruition and then I'd gone to bed early. My
phone had rung relentlessly throughout the afternoon, and I ended up turning it off. I had needed
time just for me to rest and heal as much as I
could.

As I made coffee and fed Tinker and Bell, I
glanced out the window to see the cows, Tulip and
Sunflower, eating down my grass. Both black and
white, they moved in unison. If one took a step
forward, the other did. If one lifted her head, the
other followed.

I sighed and my anger flared for a moment, but

then I realized they were saving me from mowing my yard.

"I may have to borrow them a couple times a month," I said to Belle, who had jumped on the counter and watched them with me. "If I do that, I'll never have to pull out the lawn mower again."

She meowed and began to purr. I took it as an indication that I was the smartest human she knew. Besides, I'd stopped by the grocery store on my way home yesterday and picked up her food. She must have forgiven me.

A few moments later, Minnie Johnson stalked down the driveway shaking her head as if she were really upset, but she smiled, letting me know she was mad like a parent who would get angry with a toddler who did something super cute, but a little bit naughty. As she approached her cows, I thought she should be annoyed they had the skills of Houdini, but as they nuzzled her and she stroked their heads, I could see she didn't care they'd escaped again.

The cows still had about a quarter acre to go. I also needed to interview Minnie about the fire, so maybe we could kill two birds with one stone. The rest of my lawn would get mowed and I'd get my interview.

I ran outside and down the steps just as Minnie

placed a rope around one of the cows' neck. I jogged across the lawn and the next thing I knew, I lay flat on my back, something warm seeping into my shirt.

With a groan, I sat up and saw that I'd slipped on a cow patty, then landed in it.

"Are you okay, Tilly?" Minnie asked as she ran over to me. Now that I sat closer to the ground, I noted quite a few cow presents littering my lawn. I'd forgotten how much they pooed.

"Yes. I think so."

I slowly rose to my feet and winced, while wondering if I'd cracked my tail bone as pain shot up my spine and through my hips. The cows both looked over their shoulders at me, but their jaws never stopped moving.

"I'm sorry about Sunflower and Tulip," Minnie said. "I don't know how they keep getting out. I swear I've been over every square inch of that fence and shored up anywhere that looked weak."

Wiping my hands on my jeans, I simply nodded.

"They must have seen your overgrown lawn and they couldn't help themselves."

So now her unruly cows being at my house was my fault because I hadn't pulled out my lawnmower in a month. Perfect.

Instead of letting her know my thoughts, I smiled. "I was thinking I'd interview you about the fire for an article to go into the Tri-Town Times. It would be a piece about your experience. Would that be okay?"

Her eyes widened and her mouth formed a perfect O. "Oh, my word. I would be honored. Do you need to take my picture, too? If so, I should run home and put on a little makeup."

"I'll tell you what. I need to go change. The cows can finish my lawn for me while we have coffee and talk. A picture won't be necessary."

"Okay," Minnie said hesitantly. "That will work. I don't have anything to do for the next couple of hours."

She followed me into the house and was greeted by Tinker. Belle sat on the kitchen counter and eyed Minnie from beneath hooded lids. My cat didn't like being social with anyone except me.

I went upstairs and hastily pulled off my clothes. After a quick shower, I left them in the tub and figured I'd get to them later.

When I returned to the kitchen, I found Minnie making a pot of coffee. She'd also done my dishes and swept the floor. I didn't know whether to be offended or appreciative.

"Just trying to keep busy while I waited for you," she said. "I don't like being idle for too long."

I grabbed my notebook from my purse and sat down at the table. Minnie brought me a cup of black coffee.

Yuck.

I stood and went to the fridge to pull out some cream. "Do you want any?"

"Oh, no thanks. I don't eat things like that."

Of course not.

When I sat back down, I smiled as I poured the cream into my coffee but I didn't meet her gaze. I figured I'd find a condescending stare there, and after the past couple of days, it was the last thing I needed.

"Let's get started," I said. "Tell me about your experience that night."

Minnie's recount was very different from mine.

First, she was up at one in the morning.

"I've had trouble sleeping since my son headed off to college. The house seems too big, but I don't want to move, either. So that night, I was out walking the neighborhood when the fireworks began."

I pursed my lips as I took notes and hoped she couldn't see my suspicion. I'd never been good at hiding my emotions.

"You were walking the neighborhood?" I asked for clarification, simply because I couldn't believe it.

"Yes."

Our 'neighborhood,' if you wanted to call it that, was made up of my house, and those of my three neighbors. We were surrounded by miles of farmland. My nearest neighbor besides Mr. York, Minnie, and the Ruperts lived about two miles away.

At that time of night, it wasn't people that I feared. Most were tucked away in their beds and I felt very safe in our community. But we lived at the base of a mountain, and that meant plenty of nighttime predators like coyotes, big cats, bears and wolves. It seemed beyond foolish to me for Minnie, or anyone, to be walking around after midnight.

"Did you see anyone else during your walk?" I asked.

"No," Minnie replied while shaking her head.

"So, tell me your thoughts when the fireworks went off," I said.

"My first reaction was fear, of course," she replied. "The quiet of the night had been disturbed so suddenly, and I actually thought it was a gun until the sky lit up."

A gun? Seriously? It had sounded like bombs to

me. But maybe that's because I had been fast asleep in bed, exactly where I belonged.

"The fireworks were very pretty, though," Minnie said wistfully. "I'd forgotten how beautiful they could be. I stopped right in front of Mr. York's house to watch them."

I narrowed my gaze at her, not bothering to hide my suspicions now. "You were in front of Mr. York's house?"

"That's right."

"And you didn't see anyone else?"

She shook her head. "No. I didn't even see Henry come out, which I thought was quite odd. The fireworks plainly came from his yard. I would be out of my house in a second if I were in his shoes."

"Did you know he had the fireworks?"

She nodded. "Yes, I did. I'm on the committee the mayor put together to bring back the Fourth of July celebration. He's kept it very hush-hush. He didn't want a lot of people to know about it, so it's made up of only a few of us. It was a secret, but now the cat's out of the bag, so to speak, with the fireworks going off, so I don't see any reason I can't talk about it."

I jotted down some more notes. Interesting. No one I'd talked to recently had even been aware of a mayoral committee and if anyone would have known about such a thing, it would be Debbie. She seemed to know everything about everyone's business.

The interview was supposed to be about Minnie's experience that night, but I couldn't help taking it in a different direction.

"Do you think Mr. York was out back lighting the fireworks?"

Minnie shrugged. "I suppose it's a possibility. It seems like something he'd do. Crochety old fart."

I furrowed my brow, feeling like we were talking about two different people.

"Why do you say that?" I asked.

Minnie sighed and took a sip of her coffee. "He's always yelling at me about Tulip and Sunflower. They've gotten into his yard as well, which upset him far more than it should. One time they ate his spring flower patch and he also said he hated all the cow patties they left. When I tried to explain to him how great they were for the yard and how they worked as fertilizer, he wasn't having any of it."

I found it fascinating that Minnie didn't understand what a nuisance her cows were to all of us. It was like she spoke of her unruly children, except these weighed a thousand pounds, chewed their cuds, and gave blank stares when chastised for their behavior.

"You know Mr. York is dead, right?" I asked. "That he was murdered and I found the body?"

She nodded. "I've heard, and I'm sorry you had to go through that. I can't say I'm sorry to see him go, though. Bless his soul. I hope he finds eternal peace."

The more I spoke to Minnie, the less I liked her. Could someone truly be so selfish and self-centered?

"Are you trying to solve the murder?" Minnie asked.

I shook my head. "No. Of course not. I'll leave that to the police. They're the professionals."

"That's smart, Tilly. It's probably best not to get mixed up in it."

Was that a veiled threat, or was my overactive imagination going into overdrive?

"What else do you remember from that night?" I asked, determined to get through the interview and get her out of my house.

"I heard my girls getting upset, so I ran back to my house to try and calm them down. They got out a little later in the night. Bill Rupert was outside as well, hosing down the trees located near his house. The language from that man's mouth... oh, my word!

I consider myself pretty liberal, but some of the things he was yelling, he'll definitely go straight to hell for it."

I nodded as I jotted down what she'd said. "Anything else?"

"Well, then the firetrucks pulled into your yard as well as Rupert's, and things calmed down after that."

"How did the whole experience make you feel?"

Minnie narrowed her gaze and stared into space for a moment before speaking. "Honestly, there were so many emotions. At first, fear. Then excitement. We don't get a lot of action here in Oak Peak, so when something like this happens, it's pretty interesting. Gets your heartrate up, which is always a good thing because it burns calories."

I smiled and hoped it resembled friendliness and not the fact I wanted to bury her face in one of her cows' patties.

"Did Mr. Rupert say anything to you? Did you go over and see him?"

She shook her head. "Bill Rupert is not a nice human being and we no longer speak. He had the nerve to tell me he'd put a bullet in Tulip and Sunflower and serve them up for dinner if they didn't stop going in his orchard. I can't help it if they like nectarines!"

"Okay, then!" I said, standing, unable to take anymore of Minnie's self-importance or the conversation. "I think I have everything I need."

"Oh, good. I'm so happy I could help out. When will the article be in the paper? I want to clip it and send it to my son."

"Probably Thursday."

"Great. Thank you, Tilly. I'll bring my wheel barrel over after I get the cows back on my side of the fence and clean up their messes for you."

Maybe Minnie wasn't so bad. I hadn't expected the offer. "That's very kind of you. Thank you."

"I know you're pretty klutzy. Well, with that lump on your forehead and the spill you took today, I'm surprised you haven't broken something."

She had a point, but perhaps she could have found a nicer way of saying it.

"Thanks, Minnie. Have a good day."

As I shut the door behind her, my hands began to shake. I sat down and wrote out more notes on my pad while they were still fresh.

Minnie had motive to set off the fireworks. First, she was one of the few in town who knew about them. Second, she'd get Mr. York in trouble with the police because fireworks were illegal, and that would be payback for him yelling at her about the cows. The fire in the Ruperts' yard would have been for the slight against Sunflower and Tulip, or it could have simply been an accident.

Maybe Mr. York had confronted her and she'd stabbed him. She'd certainly be stronger than him with all her exercising.

Once I had all my thoughts in order, I pulled out my laptop and wrote my piece on Minnie, leaving out my ideas about her being a murderer and sticking to her experience that night.

When Byron came over to get my statement, I'd pass on my suspicions to him. I wasn't a police officer and certainly had no business trying to solve a murder.

5

I MET MY HUSBAND, Tommy Donner, when he served at the Barksdale Airforce Base in Bosser City, Louisiana as a mechanic. While working in town as a waitress, I'd come across a lot of the military guys, but Tommy sure caught my eye—big blue eyes, black hair, thin yet muscular. That man made me laugh like no one could. He even thought my snorting was cute.

He then retired from the Air Force due to an injury he received while working on one of the jets. When he sliced off part of his thumb, they gave him the option of retirement, and he took it.

After we'd been dating about a year, he begged me to move to Oak Peak with him. He'd grown up there and wanted to return even though his parents had both passed. I didn't care about the waitressing job, but I had also landed a part time gig at the local paper doing light editing, some ad sales, and writing "fluff" pieces. I was left with a decision: Did I choose love, or a job I adored?

Well, obviously, I chose love.

Tommy and I were married shortly after we moved to Oak Peak. We saved up our money and bought the big farmhouse I lived in with expectations of bringing in lots of animals and having a couple of kids. It had been vacant for a few years, but both of us saw its potential. While Tommy managed the hardware store in Little River, I concentrated on making our house a home. I sewed curtains, painted, and scrubbed the floors until they looked like new. It took months, but we had a beautiful home that I loved. Life was really, really good.

I grew up in the small town of Hesston, Kansas until the age of ten when my father died suddenly of a heart attack. Shortly after, we moved to Louisiana where my mom met my stepfather, who I loved dearly. We lived on the bayou, and my small-town upbringing gave me excellent knowledge of small town politics.

My mama always told me there was a distinct difference between someone being nice and someone being friendly. When someone was nice, they smiled and spoke pleasantly, but they'd think twice about getting their shoes wet if they saw you drowning in a lake. A friendly person really cared, and they'd dive in headfirst to save you.

People in Oak Peak were nice to me when I first arrived, but I knew deep down none of them were friendly. If they'd seen me struggling to stay afloat in a lake, they'd probably have pulled up a chair and taken bets on how long I'd last.

And I'd been okay with that, because I knew in time they'd grow to like me. It was the small-town way: caution, followed by trust, followed by friendship.

Tommy and I had tried for a baby for just under a year but failed. I saw a big city doctor and was told kids wouldn't be in my future unless we adopted. This devastated both of us, but we worked past it and I thought we were happy. To this day, I still can't believe I didn't see the signs. Working late. Leaving early. Our love life took a deep dive. Finally, he left me for a waitress at a bar in Little River. And to really dig the knife in my back... she was pregnant.

Tommy actually felt guilty about his infidelity and left me the house without asking for a red cent. That had been a year ago.

I strongly considered heading back home to the Louisiana, but when the town found out about Tommy leaving me for the pregnant waitress, things changed. Sure, I'd made a couple of friends in my two years of living there, but I was still considered an outsider. This was never said to me, but I could feel it in my bones. The people of Oak Peak were tough to crack. When Tommy left, most rallied around me, ashamed that one of their own would do such a horrible thing. Some brought me meals. Harold offered me a job. Debbie down at the bakery started gossiping with me, instead of initiating the "nice" talk, and she quickly became one of my besties. I was finally one of them, so I decided to stay. I missed my parents, but I had worked too hard to leave the house that I loved, where I had dumped my sweat and tears to make it my home.

Tommy leaving and his unfaithfulness hurt more than I could have imagined. I became so lonely I couldn't sleep at night, so I adopted Tinker and Belle. They actually made me feel a little bit better and taking care of them kept my mind off the man.

Seven months after Tommy's departure, I was fully divorced. Signing the documents was one of the hardest things I'd ever had to do, and I found it easier to ignore them than to actually put the pen to paper. Then, one day, I guess I'd just had enough. It hit me that Tommy wasn't coming back and he had a new family. I finally signed and mentioned it to Debbie, who apparently let everyone in town know. The ink hadn't even dried on the paper and Deputy Byron Mills swooped in and asked me out.

Unfortunately, I'd said yes. There wasn't anything wrong with him; he just didn't do anything for me. Admittedly, I found him a bit stupid.

I sighed when I saw his sheriff's car coming down my driveway. It was time to give my statement, so I decided to make it quick and keep it professional. No tears from me today. I'd say my piece and get him out of my home.

Byron slid out the car when I opened the front door. Tinker bound down the steps to go greet him, her tail wagging so hard, I was surprised she didn't throw out her back. Byron gave her a couple scratches under the chin and she took off around the yard. He waved to me, then opened the door to the back seat and emerged with a cage covered in a sheet.

As he approached, a large grin spread over his face. "I brought you a present!"

I stared at the cage, then heard its inhabitants.

Cluck. Cluck. Cluck.

"You brought me... chickens?"

"Yes!"

I tucked a lock of hair behind my ear and shook my head. "Byron, what am I going to do with chickens?"

"Well, I thought you could enjoy the eggs. You've got that old coop out back. After I get your statement, I thought I'd shore it up for you, clean it out, and get them moved in."

Clamping shut my unhinged jaw, I tried to appreciate the gesture. We didn't have chickens down on the bayou because they would be an invitation for gators. I'd never had contact with the animals except for the ones on my dinner plate.

"Okay, well, thank you," I said as we entered the house, but I wasn't sure I meant it.

After he pulled up the sheet, the two brown hens eyed me through the wiring. Maybe they would be a nice addition, and I did love eggs.

"The feed store had them up for adoption," Byron said as he placed them on the kitchen table. "I immediately thought of you when I saw them."

So Byron associated chickens with me. How? Why? I wasn't sure how I felt about that.

One of them ruffled her feathers. Dust and who-knew-what-else flew all over. "I'm going to put them outside," I said. "It seems a little dirty to have them on the table where I eat."

After I set them down on the porch, I grabbed some spray cleaner and paper towels and wiped down the table surface. Then, we both took a chair.

"How are you holding up, Tilly?" Byron asked as he reached across the table and grabbed my hand, his gaze shining with concern. "I've been worried about you."

It seemed that if I stayed busy, I could keep my mind off Mr. York, and I'd been very busy interviewing Minnie and writing my piece for the paper. I also felt like my insides vibrated with excitement because I couldn't wait to tell Byron my suspicions on her.

"I'm okay," I replied. "I'm looking forward to giving my statement and being done with it."

Thankfully, he received my not-so-subtle hint and pulled out a pad of paper from his back pocket.

The Tri-Town area had pulled together their collective resources and formed one Sheriff's Department that serviced all three towns. Mike Connor, the Sheriff, oversaw six deputies, including Byron.

"Tell me what happened yesterday morning, Tilly."

I quickly recounted my story, eager to get to the good part about Minnie, but Byron kept questioning me.

"Why were you there in the first place? Did you stop by Mr. York's place in the morning a lot?"

"Of course not," I replied, furrowing my brow. "I wanted to know what he said to you after I left that night."

Byron eyed me but remained silent.

"What?"

"Are you sure you weren't having relations with him? I find it odd for you to be at his home at seven in the morning."

"Oh, jeez, Byron," I said, rolling my eyes. "That's the stupidest thing I've ever heard you say."

I fidgeted in my seat as he stared at me.

"Byron, I swear to you, I wasn't having an affair with Mr. York. That's just silly."

"Okay, then," he said with a nod. "Is there anything we haven't discussed?"

For a moment, I hesitated answering because I just wanted him out of my house. Did he really think I could have an affair with Mr. York, or was he questioning me to see if I was dating someone else? But my duty to be a good citizen overrode my anger at his antics, so I decided to tell him about Minnie.

"Yes. Before he died, Mr. York told me the killer and the person who lit off the fireworks are one and the same."

Byron's eyes widened. "Really?"

"And, I had an interesting conversation with Minnie Johnson. She lives kitty-corner from me and behind Mr. York."

"What did she have to say?"

"She's got the motive to light the fireworks *and* to kill Mr. York, especially if he confronted her about setting off the fireworks. And, she knew they were there because she's on the mayor's committee to bring back the Fourth of July celebration."

As I explained my theory, Byron took more notes.

"I think you may want to really look into that," I concluded.

"The Sheriff's Department doesn't know about any committee. Are you sure it's true?"

Or maybe you *just don't know about it*.

"I'm only telling you what Minnie said to me. I can't verify the committee, but it seems like a good bet that there is one. The mayor asked Mr. York to hold the fireworks for him, and then Minnie said the mayor wanted to keep the committee a secret. Only a few people knew. So, yeah, I think the mayor has a committee."

"And you think Minnie murdered Mr. York?"

"I don't know, Byron," I said with a sigh. "I'm just saying that if she did, it fits."

"Are you working to solve these cases?" he asked as he narrowed his gaze on me. "Who lit the fireworks and who killed York?"

"No! That's ridiculous! I have no business trying to solve a murder. I'll gladly leave that to the police... the professionals."

"Good," Byron said, closing his notebook. His demeanor had changed. He no longer looked at me as if concerned, but instead, wariness hung in his gaze. "Civilians have no place in police business."

"Of course not. I don't know the first thing about finding a killer."

Our stares locked for a moment and he gazed at me as if he didn't believe me.

"Really, Byron. I'm just passing on information I learned."

"I'll head out back and fix that coop now," he said with a nod.

When I opened the front door, I found Tinker lying down next to the chickens, her nose pressed up against the cage and her tail wagging.

"Looks like she's made some new friends," Byron said with a laugh.

He carried the hens around the side of the house with Tinker trailing after him.

I wondered what I had said that caused the change in Byron. We'd started the conversation with him being concerned for me and ended it with him giving me suspicious looks.

Why?

Was he still thinking I could be having relations with Mr. York, or didn't he like me sharing my thoughts on Minnie?

I sighed and decided not to fret over it too much. A man who brings a woman chickens as a gift shouldn't worry me.

Besides, he was the one with the murder to solve, not me.

I was only trying to help.

6

HAVING a murderer in town had given me the willies. I didn't sleep very well and found myself reaching for Tinker and Belle multiple times through the night. Tinker would let me know if something wasn't right in the house, but the question was, what would I do then? My dog was a lover, not a fighter. If someone broke into my home, she'd be the first one out.

The next day, even though I ran on very little sleep, my morning routine went smoothly. I'd risen a little earlier to feed the chickens. Byron had left some food for them, but I needed more. I made a mental note to stop by the Filly Feed.

Still unsure if I wanted the hens, I stared at them and they glared back at me. Tinker, however, seemed very pleased with the new additions. She sat by their cage wagging her tail. I hadn't let her beyond their fencing because I wasn't sure if she really wanted to make friends or eat them.

"Okay, you two," I said. "I'm coming in to change the water. Be nice."

I slipped through the gate and the hens strutted around me clucking away. Then both attacked my legs, each pecking me harder than the last.

"Ouch!" I yelled, bending down to shoo them away, but they were relentless. "Knock it off!"

My pain seemed to only fuel them on, and I quickly exited while making a mental note I'd need to wear jeans when feeding them from now on.

"I'd hoped we'd get along better than this," I said. "We play nice around here, so you two better learn some manners."

Once I'd retrieved them fresh water, I grabbed my keys and headed to work. Yellow crime scene tape had been strung across Mr. York's drive. They apparently didn't want anyone near his house and a wave of sadness washed over me once again. I would miss my neighbor.

As I pulled up in front of the paper, I debated whether a donut would do me good, or not.

"That would be a hard no," I mumbled as I slid

out of my truck and concentrated on the door leading to the Tri-Town Times muttering *no donuts* as I went.

"Good morning, Tilly!" Harold boomed when I walked in. "Loved the piece on Minnie Johnson. Really heartfelt."

"'Morning," I muttered, throwing him a glance. His eyes danced with excitement and I don't think I'd ever seen him that enthusiastic. "Glad you liked it."

"So I was thinking about what you should write today," he said. "We've still got a lot to cross out on our list. What piece do you think will make the biggest impact?"

I glanced down at my notes.

Interview Ruperts and Minnie for humanity piece.

Interview mayor about fireworks.

Interview police about murder.

As I crossed off Minnie, I considered my other two options. The mayor's interview would be a little more hard-hitting than the one with the Ruperts. Besides, I'd have to confront him about the fireworks and his secret committee Minnie had mentioned, and the thought of questioning an elected official made my stomach turn. I didn't know if I had the fortitude to do so.

I should probably save the police until they had time to process the evidence and information they had gathered.

"The ad money is rolling in like nothing I've ever seen," Harold said. "I know this crime affected you personally, but it has the whole town talking. They can't wait to get their hands on the paper. Letters to the Editor are coming in—so many I won't be able to print them all."

I nodded, still staring at my list.

"One other thing," Tilly," Harold said, his voice turning somber.

"What's that?"

"Do you want to write the obituary for York?"

I sighed and rubbed my forehead. "I didn't really know him. I mean, I *knew* him, but I wasn't even aware of his first name until after he died. We talked a bit here and there, but in a neighborly way. We weren't close."

"Do you know any of his kin?"

"Nope. I know he was a widower. I don't know if he had kids. If so, I don't recall them ever coming to visit."

"Very sad," Harold said, furrowing his brow. "Maybe we can track them down if the police haven't already. I'm sure they'd notify the children."

We stared at each other a beat, then I made my decision. Just talking about the dead drained me. I needed to concentrate on the living. "I'm going to talk to the Ruperts today."

Frankly, interviewing the mayor and the police seemed a little daunting. Going from writing about bake sales to questioning those in authority was a huge jump for me.

"Sounds good. Since the mayor is such a busy man, I'll see if I can get you an appointment for the interview sometime in the next few days."

"Okay. I'll go see the Ruperts in a little bit after I run a couple of errands."

Harold's phone began to ring, and I picked up the stack of mail. As I sorted it into piles of junk, ad money, and letters to the editor, I noticed that we had some mail intended for the florist, as well as the bakery. I took them and headed out, dropping the florist letters through the mail slot, then I walked over to Debbie's Deliciousness.

"Tilly!" she called from behind the counter. "Come here, girl!"

I stepped toward her as she approached me and gave me a big bear hug. "Some of your mail came to the paper," I said. "I've got it for you here."

Debbie shook her head as she took it from me. "I

heard there's a new sorter at the post office trying to fill Phillip's shoes while he recovers from his appendectomy. The poor girl doesn't do the job very well. You're the third person who brought me my mail in the past few days."

She glanced around the store to make sure the other three customers weren't paying us any attention, then leaned in to whisper in my ear. "I've got news for you."

"What?"

"Let me get us some coffee. Go sit down."

When we were situated, she leaned forward as I poured cream into my cup. "I was talking to someone... who it was isn't important. But they said they'd heard from someone whose cousin works at City Hall that the mayor was getting pushback about reviving the Fourth of July fireworks celebration."

"From who? Who was fighting it?"

"You know Betty Frank down at the feed store?"

I nodded and took a sip from my cup. The liquid burned my tongue but tasted wonderful.

"She was asked to be on a secret Fourth of July committee the mayor had formed but started to feel guilty about it because she remembers the fire. She had a big shouting match with the mayor in his office that she was going to expose him and his celebration plans."

"Did you know about the committee?" I asked.

Debbie shook her head. "They did a good job of keeping it a secret."

"Until now."

"Yes, until now. With the fireworks going off, there isn't a secret to keep. Everyone is revealing what they knew and when."

"What did the mayor say to Betty when she confronted him?"

"He told her she'd regret it if she did, and he was in charge of this town. Like no one should mess with him."

Debbie stared at me expectantly, her gaze dancing with excitement. I had a feeling I was supposed to connect the dots and come up with some huge surprise, but I couldn't.

"What does all that mean?" I asked.

Debbie sighed and rolled her eyes. "You're not much of a reporter, are you?"

"That's not very nice," I said, my feelings truly hurt.

"Think about it, Tilly. This is a huge story!"

I sipped my coffee and desperately tried to fit the puzzle pieces together.

"I write about your new flavor of donuts or the sewing club," I finally said. "All of this is way out of my league."

"Okay, listen up." Debbie glanced around her store once again. "What if the mayor was the one to light the fireworks? He and his committee were the only ones who knew they were on Henry York's land. What if he felt the pushback, feared being exposed, and wanted to get rid of them, then accused Henry of lighting them? That way, he'd emerge with his hands clean."

I tossed her theory around for a minute, and it made sense.

Oak Peak residents, especially those who had been around for a long time, remember the fire and the aftermath of rebuilding the town. If it had gotten out that the mayor wanted to bring back the fireworks, there would have been a lot of angry people.

That didn't bode well for re-election.

But then I remembered what Mr. York had said right before he died.

"Who killed Mr. York?" I asked. "He said it was the same person who lit the fireworks."

"Well, obviously that sneaky turd, Mayor Douglas Shelton!"

"How do you make that jump?"

"Oh, Tilly. What am I going to do with you? The mayor went by the next day and told York he had lit them, but York had to take the fall. The old man said he wouldn't do it, no matter how friendly he'd been with Shelton's daddy. They fought and the mayor won."

If that were the case, that totally destroyed my theory of Minnie lighting the fireworks and killing Mr. York. Or maybe she had been in cahoots with the mayor and they'd worked together to commit both crimes.

Maybe the mayor was having an affair with Minnie.

"That's a really interesting theory," I said, my heartbeat picking up with excitement. "The mayor probably thinks he's above the law and he can get away with it."

"Right," Debbie said, nodding. "That's exactly it. Who's going to suspect the guy who actually runs the town of such awful deeds?"

I finished my coffee and stood. "Thanks for the info, Debbie. I'll pass it on to the police."

"Glad to help," she said, giving me a hug goodbye.

So now I'd uncovered two theories—or three if I

took into consideration that Minnie and the mayor were working together.

As I walked down the street toward the feed store, I decided to confirm that Betty Frank, the owner, was going to expose Mayor Shelton.

Besides, I needed chicken feed.

I pulled open the store door and accidentally hit myself in the nose with it. Usually, doors were so much heavier and required a little more strength to open. Apparently, not this one.

"Oh, my goodness!" Betty yelled as she ran over. "Are you okay?"

I nodded as I held my nose, pretty sure it wasn't broken, but good Lord above did it hurt. "I'm fine. Just a little klutzy."

Betty was older than me by about fifteen years, which put her in her fifties. Her hair had gone gray, and she wore it in a long ponytail. With her pointed nose, wide brown eyes and thin face, she reminded me of a hawk.

"Have you been in before?" she asked. "I don't recall ever seeing you."

In my two years of living in Oak Peak, I'd never stepped foot into the Filly Feed. I didn't have any livestock, so there was no need for me to enter. I bought the dog and cat food at the grocery store... when I could remember to do so.

"No," I said. "I'm Tilly Donner."

She narrowed her gaze at me as if trying to place the name. After a few seconds, her whole face lit up in surprise.

"Of course! You write for the paper! And your husband... "

Her sentence trailed off as she realized what she was about to say.

"Yes," I said, "he left me after impregnating a waitress."

"I'm- I'm sorry about that," she stammered, obviously uncomfortable. "What can I do for you?"

"Well, Deputy Mills brought me some chickens, and I need some feed."

"Wasn't that sweet of him?" she asked, then motioned for me to follow her. "Such a nice man."

Frankly, I would have preferred flowers. For starters, they didn't bite and peck. But I remained quiet.

"I see your name in the paper all the time," she called from the back room. "You do a nice job of reporting the news in our little slice of heaven."

"Thank you," I murmured as I studied my reflection in a steel dog bowl. I had a cut on the bridge of my nose that had already scabbed. Between that, the bump on my forehead, and the scratches on my legs thanks to the chickens, I looked like I'd been in a boxing match... and lost.

Betty emerged with a sack that read *Chicken Feed* across the front. "Do you need antibiotics as well?"

"I didn't know I had to have any."

"Oh, yes. And we also carry a vitamin formula that helps with egg production."

Considering I wasn't even certain I wanted to keep them, I was sure about to spend a lot of money.

"Just the feed for now."

As she rang me up, I tried to figure out how to engage her about the secret fireworks committee. Finally, I decided to just ask.

"I heard around town that you were on a committee the mayor put together to bring back the Fourth of July fireworks."

Her cheeks turned crimson and she wouldn't meet my stare for a moment. When she did finally look at me, I saw anger.

"Are you reporting on this for the paper? If so, I have no idea what you're talking about. No comment, or whatever they say."

"No, I'm not reporting on it. It's just something I heard. If it makes a difference, I think you did the right thing. Fireworks don't belong in a town like this, especially after all the destruction they caused before."

Her gaze shifted all around the store before she spoke. "Well, thank you. Yes, I thought it was wrong. I remember the fire and it was horrible. I couldn't imagine putting the town through something like that again. Just don't be writing anything about me in the paper. I like to keep my business to myself."

"No worries," I replied. "Thanks for helping me with the feed."

Well, I'd confirmed the pushback on the mayor, and it only made Debbie's theory more believable.

Maybe the mayor was responsible? I'd have to pass it on to Byron because I couldn't imagine the police not wanting to know everything I uncovered.

Surely, it would help them solve the murder.

7

AFTER THE FEED STORE, I stopped by the Grocery Barn to pick up a few things. As I stood in the cookie aisle trying to make my choice, a little voice in the back of my mind told me to skip it. I'd already done so well bypassing the donut, and did I *really* need cookies? I hurried out of the store, cookie-free and feeling proud of my decision.

Before calling Byron, I placed a call to Bill and Sharon Rupert. Even though they'd lived behind me for two years, we'd never been really friendly. I hardly ever saw them because the orchard separated my house from theirs. I also rarely noticed them around town. Now and again I'd see them tending to the trees by my house, and we'd wave at each other, but that was it. When Tommy and I had first moved in, they'd come over, introduced themselves, brought us some nectarine jam, and left their number. I'd been so embarrassed because I'd locked myself out of the house and had to fetch the emergency key from under a potted plant in order to take the jam inside and offer them some tea.

The jam had been delicious and I'd admired Sharon's ability to make something so amazing. I wasn't bad in the kitchen, but that jelly tasted like it had been created by angels and dropped down directly from heaven.

"Hello?"

"Hey, Sharon, it's Tilly Donner."

"Oh, my word! Hello, Tilly! What can I do for you?"

"Well, I'm writing up a piece for the Tri-Town Times about the fire. My boss wanted me to see if you and Bill would be willing to talk to me and tell me about your experience that night."

A brief pause hung in the air and I thought I heard voices in the background. "Let me ask if he wants to do that. Hang on."

As she talked to her husband, I couldn't make out what they said. But then I heard another female voice.

Sharon returned. "Yes, I guess that would be okay," she said.

"Okay, great. I've got to stop by the house to drop off my groceries, then I'll just walk over through the orchard."

"All right. Just be careful. I don't want to see you hurt. The ground's a bit unsteady after the fire and there may be hot patches."

"I will, thanks."

Once home, I found Tinker outside lying next to the chickens again, her nose stuffed between the wiring. One of the chickens actually pecked at her, and she seemed to like it because her tail swished back and forth lazily.

"Hey, Tinker!" I called. She glanced up at me, then jammed her nose back into the coop. The chicken began pecking her again.

Was my dog falling in love with the hens?

I carried my paper bags inside and Belle came out from the living room to say hello, strutting in between my legs as I tried not to trip over her. It wouldn't have been the first time.

"Hang on, Belly-Belle," I said. "Let me put these down. Please don't send me to the floor. I've already got this knot on my head, my butt hurts, and my legs look like I went head-to-head with a wayward razor and lost."

She meowed but let me pass.

After setting down the bags, I picked her up and walked to the back of the house. Both of us stared at Tinker while I pet her.

"I don't know what's got into that dog," I murmured. "She's just lying there allowing those stupid birds to peck her nose."

Belle meowed through her purring.

We watched a few more minutes, then I went back to the kitchen and set Belle back down. "Sorry, girl. I've got to put the groceries away and then head over to the Ruperts. As much as I'd like to curl up on the couch with you and watch *Judge Judy*, someone has to pay our bills."

Belle found a slice of sunlight, plopped down on the floor, and stretched out, her purring becoming louder. Sometimes I wished I was a cat.

Specifically, *my* cat.

I quickly put away the groceries then walked out across my land, slipped through the fence to the Ruperts' property, and felt like I was entering another world.

The orchard had been planted in an orderly

fashion—rows with equal space between the trees. It made for easy traveling toward their home.

The bare, black limbs stretched toward me like claws. The air suddenly felt different... quiet, like death. Even though I could hear the birds chirping, I didn't see any. They must have been perched on something alive.

As I made my way through the carnage, I finally saw greenery and picked up my pace. The first three rows of trees closest to the house were the only ones that survived.

When I emerged from the orchard, I debated whether I should walk around the house and use the front door, which would be proper, or just knock on the back. I crossed a small, grassy backyard, and ascended the steps to the back door, which happened to be sliding glass.

I could see straight through the living room to the front door. To my surprise, I spotted Sharon giving Betty Frank from the feed store a hug.

I had no idea they were friends, but then again, I didn't really socialize with either of them.

Bill Rupert came into my line of vision. Tall and thin with a head full of gray hair, he grinned as he opened the door.

"Hey, Tilly," he said. "Welcome."

"Hi, there."

"Come on in and sit down. We just put on a pot of coffee. Would you like some?"

"That would be great. Thank you."

"Cream? Sugar?"

I almost said both, but then I remembered I was thinking about losing weight. "I'll just go with the cream, please."

As I followed him into the kitchen, I glanced around the house. Done in tans and deep browns, I found it a bit drab. It reminded me of my own house. Tommy had picked out the paint colors and I hadn't fought him.

"Have a seat," he said, pointing at the kitchen table. The décor in that space was definitely more colorful, consisting of red and blue chickens. I wondered if the Ruperts would be interested in adopting my hens. I figured if they actually wallpapered their kitchen with chickens, they must like them.

Sharon entered a moment later. "Hi, Tilly."

"Hi. Was that Betty from the feed store I saw leaving?"

"Sure was. She's just been a doll throughout this whole ordeal. We've been good friends for years."

I nodded as the two sat down. Bill set my cup in

front of me—white porcelain with blue chickens. The Ruperts were definitely a candidate for adopting the hens.

"You said you want to interview us about the fire," Bill said.

"Yes. It's a piece for the paper on the human aspects of the fire, about your loss."

Sharon's eyes welled and she quickly looked down at the table. "It's been so difficult."

"I know, honey," Bill said, patting her hand. "We're going to be just fine. We'll bounce back."

"Can you please tell me about what happened?"

"Well, I was up reading and thought the end of the world was near," Sharon said, shaking her head. "I don't think I've ever been so terrified."

"You were awake at one in the morning?" I asked. Why were all my neighbors such night owls?

"Yes. I have insomnia. Some nights I'm up until very late."

"I keep telling her to see a doctor about it, but she won't," Bill said with a sigh. "But that night was very scary."

"Once we realized the orchard was on fire, we sprang into action," Sharon continued. "I called the fire department then ran outside to start the hose."

"Since Sharon was already up, she beat me out

there. The heat from the flames made me think we'd walked right into the gates of Hell," Bill said. "Horrible heat."

"Did you ever think it was too dangerous? That maybe you should leave and let the fire department take over?"

"Oh, no," Bill replied. "We had to save any trees we could. Besides, I wouldn't allow my home to be destroyed."

I jotted down my notes, trying to imagine watching my property, my livelihood, burn.

"Where do you sell your nectarines?" I asked.

"The Tri-Town grocery stores are our biggest client, followed by us selling them at the fair. We also ship some down to the southern part of the state."

"So, this is really going to affect you," I replied, feeling so sorry for them, tears stung my eyes.

Bill waved his hand in front of his face as if to wipe away my statement. "I've still got my job at the tractor shop. We're going to be fine."

Sharon smiled quietly, but I saw doubt in her eyes. Their finances weren't any of my business, so I let the matter drop.

"I'm glad to hear it."

I took a few more notes as I considered how to write the article.

"Do you know why York would have lit them?" Sharon asked.

I glanced up from my paper pad. "He didn't."

"How do you know that?" Sharon asked as she furrowed her brow.

"He told me. You know he's dead, right?"

Both nodded somberly.

"May he find eternal peace." Sharon said, closing her eyes. "Amen."

"Amen. I found him just before he died, and he told me the person who lit the fireworks was the same as the person who murdered him."

"You poor girl," Sharon said. "What an awful thing for you."

Bill shook his head in disgust. "Such tragedy to hit our little part of the world. First the fire, then the murder. I hope it isn't true that bad things happen in threes. I can't imagine what could be next."

A chill went down my spine. Hopefully that would be the end of the bad events because the only two people in our area who hadn't been horribly affected by the happenings that night were Minnie and me. If bad things did happen in threes, there was a fifty-fifty chance I'd be next.

Just then, I heard a cow. All three of us glanced out the window to see Tulip and Sunflower in the orchard, munching on nectarines.

Bill cursed with such force, he startled me as he stood and knocked over his chair. Now, being married to a military man, I'd heard more than my fair share of colorful language, but the stuff that came out of Bill's mouth actually made me blush.

I grabbed my notepad and Sharon and I followed him out to the back door.

"Get out of here, you slabs of meat!" he yelled.

Tulip and Sunflower stared at him without moving.

He pulled a phone from his pocket and quickly dialed, then held it up to his ear. "Minnie, get over here and get these damn cows off my property! This is your last warning! If they come over again, I'll shoot them!"

After shoving the phone back in his pocket, he turned to me. "Pardon my French back there. I've been fighting these cows for months and Minnie treats them like they're her own kids. It's terribly frustrating for me."

"Frankly, I don't blame you," I replied. "I'd be angry as well."

A few moments later, Minnie stomped across her

yard and into the Ruperts'. I could see where the cows had come through the fence. The top two wooden slats had fallen, each hanging by a single nail. The cows must have leaned on it, then simply stepped over the bottom slat to enter the orchard.

"How dare you threaten my babies like that!" Minnie yelled. "You cranky coot! I can't help it if they like nectarines, and if you hurt my cows, I'll put a knife in you while you're sleeping!"

"I'd really like to see you try that, you crazy, cow-loving kook!"

An interesting threat considering Mr. York had just died by stabbing. I jotted it down in my notebook.

As the two continued to yell at each other, Sharon slipped back into the house and I decided to head home. Watching people argue and call each other names made me anxious.

I sighed with relief as I walked through the orchard and their voices faded.

When I arrived home, I checked on the chicken coop and found Tinker still getting her nose pecked, then went inside.

I plopped down on the couch and Belle came to sit on me. As I slowly stroked her back, I called Byron.

"What's up, Tilly?" he asked.

"I have another theory for you on who killed Mr. York and lit the fireworks."

"Do you, now?"

"Yes."

"Let's hear it."

As I repeated Debbie's idea, the more I liked it. It seemed like the most viable option: the mayor had lit the shed full of fireworks to get rid of the evidence and blamed Mr. York. They argued, and the mayor killed him.

"That's interesting," Byron said.

"I thought so. It makes sense. But then Minnie Johnson just said she'd put a knife in Bill Rupert if he hurt Tulip and Sunflower."

"Those two are at it again?"

"Yep. Just witnessed it all with my own eyes. You should look into her as well. You've got two good leads on who killed Mr. York."

Byron made some non-committed sound, and then said he had to go.

I hung up and picked up Belle off my lap and set her on the couch. She glared at me, letting me know she hadn't been done with me.

"Sorry, girl. I have an article to write."

After grabbing my laptop from the kitchen, I sat on the sofa again.

I'd handed the police really good scenarios that explained Mr. York's death and the fireworks.

When would an arrest be made? I couldn't wait to see which one of the theories was correct.

8

THE NEXT DAY, I went to the office and once again skipped my donut. It took a thirty-five hundred calorie deficit to lose a pound. I had no idea how many I had cut not having my donuts, but I felt really good about myself and my choices. I had to be getting slimmer.

"Hey, Harold."

"Tilly! Excellent work on the Rupert story."

"Thanks," I replied as I went through the mail. Once again, we had letters that didn't belong to us. "I heard that Philip down at the post office had an appendectomy and someone else is filling in for him. Whoever it is doesn't do a very good job. We've got more mail that isn't ours."

"Hopefully he'll return soon. Maybe there's a

story there as well: Town in Uproar Over Incompetent Mail Sorter."

I rolled my eyes, unsure if he was joking. "I'm not going to drag someone through the mud for not organizing the mail right."

Harold laughed and tossed his pen on the desk. "We're getting great feedback on your articles and ad revenue is through the roof."

"Glad to hear it."

"I also got you an interview at eleven today with the mayor. He only has twenty minutes, so make sure your questions are clear and concise."

My stomach flipped as I sat down at my desk. I didn't feel qualified to do the job. Fundraisers and business spotlights were more my speed.

"Do you want some help on what you should ask him?"

"I would appreciate it."

"Come over here."

I dragged my chair over to his desk and sat down next to him. He pulled a pad of paper from his drawer, and I realized I hadn't shared Debbie's theory about how the mayor could be involved in the murder.

Once I told him about it, he tapped his pencil on the desk and stared off into space.

After a moment, he said, "This makes a difference on how we're going to approach this. I was thinking we'd do a softball interview, but we better step up our game. If even a quarter of what you told me is true, he's got to explain himself to his constituents."

I squirmed in my chair as he scratched out some notes.

"You can do this," he said. "I know it's a step up for you, but just remember the mayor is human. He doesn't have superpowers. He doesn't wear a cape. He can't melt you with lasers coming out of his eyes. The only thing that's intimidating is the fact that he can call himself the leader of our small town."

"And that he may have killed someone."

"Well, yes. There's that as well. He's not going to bother you though. What do you think he'll do? Jump across his desk and stab you with a pen?"

I giggled as I tried to picture the scenario. "More like try to staple my mouth shut."

We both laughed as Harold continued to write. A minute later, he handed me a slip of paper with questions on it. "Grab your notepad and go get 'em, tiger!"

As I left, I felt more like a lamb to the slaughter,

but I threw my shoulders back and walked the couple blocks to City Hall.

I can do this.

The big white building housed most of the local government entities: the police department, the city council, and the mayor's office. It sat in the middle of a huge, pretty grassy area smattered with oak and cherry trees and the main road separated and went around it. When the trees bloomed, it was gorgeous.

I found the directory to the left of the big rotunda lobby and noted the mayor's office was on the third floor.

Stairs or elevator?

The stairs would be a smart option for exercise, but I wouldn't end up winded on the elevator. I decided for the stairs since I'd been so good at making healthy decisions for myself.

When I got to the top, I took a moment to catch my breath. I certainly didn't want to meet the mayor while gasping for air.

I pushed open the door to his office. The secretary smiled as I introduced myself.

"Have a seat. He'll be with you shortly."

I sat in the black leather chair as the secretary returned to her typing. The sound of her nails clicking on the keyboard was irritating—like someone scratching a chalkboard. Hopefully, I wouldn't be sitting in her presence for too much longer.

Trying to imagine Betty Frank from Filly Feed yelling at the mayor about the fireworks in the small office was easy. With the main door to his office open, the conversation would have carried throughout this floor, and maybe onto the first and second with the open lobby. I'd be shocked if there weren't more people who'd heard the confrontation.

As I waited, I glanced around the small room. Besides the secretary's black desk, there was a matching credenza behind her and a small bookcase in front of me, also black. Thankfully, the credenza sat below a window and it allowed for some light to come in. Otherwise, the place would be dank and dark. I'd hate to work in it.

Five minutes turned into fifteen.

"Excuse me," I said. "My appointment was at eleven and now it's a quarter after."

"He'll be with you shortly," she said with a sniff.

I studied her blonde bob, pointed nose, and the reading glasses perched on the bridge. Even though I pegged her to be a few years younger than me, she seemed older, like life had aged her beyond her years. I noted she also wore a black blazer with a white shirt. The mayor must prefer the color.

After another ten minutes, I stood and walked over to the desk.

"Please back up," the secretary said, pushing her chair away from me.

"I'm only wondering when I can see the mayor," I said. "I have an appointment. Is he always running this far behind?"

"Please, sit down!"

I backed away from the desk and held my hands up to my shoulders as if her words were a weapon and I surrendered. What went on in this office? Was she threatened on a regular basis?

"Fine," I said. "I'm only wondering when I can talk to him."

The paper in my pocket with all the questions burned like it had caught on fire and I had a sinking feeling I wouldn't get to ask them.

"He'll call you when he's ready! I already told you that!"

I rolled my eyes and sat down. What a drama queen. Would I actually get a chance to talk to the mayor, or not?

My guess fell in the *no* column the longer I waited.

Five minutes later, I startled when the door to the mayor's office flew open and he stormed into the waiting room.

"I'll be back soon, Cheryl," he boomed as he passed me and pulled a phone out of his pocket.

I quickly stood. "Excuse me, Mayor! We had an appointment a half hour ago! I need to talk to you!"

He glanced over his shoulder with a furrowed brow. "I'm late. Schedule something with Cheryl."

"But I already did!" I yelled. "For a half-hour ago!"

Anger flooded through me and I fisted my hands at my sides. I'd been patiently waiting for him, and I couldn't help but think he'd allowed my interview time to slip away because he didn't want to answer any questions. I may not like conflict, but I wouldn't tolerate being brushed aside.

Before he fully exited the office, I decided to at least get one question in. "Mayor Shelton, is it true that you're responsible for putting the fireworks on Mr. York's land?"

He stopped dead in his tracks, then slowly turned to me. His mouth set in a fine line and his brow furrowed in fury.

"Excuse me?"

"Mr. York told me that you asked him to hide the

fireworks. Is that the truth? And if so, why would you want to bring back something that once destroyed this town?"

He pulled on the lapels of his suit as he glared at me. "I've already told you you'll need to schedule something with Cheryl. I've got places to be."

"And I told you that I had an appointment, so the least you could do is answer my question."

Honestly, my bravery surprised me, especially since I'd been so nervous about coming to see the mayor. However, I didn't like being ignored.

He took two steps toward me, his cheeks reddened. "Yes, I was the one who bought the fireworks with the intent of bringing them back into some sort Fourth of July celebration. I asked York to keep them for me. Is there anything else?"

"Is it true you were getting pushback from some members of your secret Fourth of July committee?"

"I have no idea what you're talking about."

"Did you light the fireworks?" I shot back.

"That's enough," Cheryl said as she hurried over and placed herself between me and the mayor. "Run along now, Doug. I'll take care of this one."

Like I was some type of bug that needed to be squashed. The mayor left without another word.

"You listen to me, you frumpy toad," Cheryl said,

wagging her perfectly manicured red fingernail in front of my face. "You stay away from my husband with your silly questions. He had nothing to do with the tragedy that happened out there."

I had no idea Cheryl was the mayor's wife, but my anger hadn't simmered down quite yet, and I felt a little mouthy, especially after the insult.

"Did you know people are saying that he not only lit the fireworks, which destroyed the Ruperts' orchard, but killed Mr. York as well?"

"That's utterly ridiculous. Silly gossip by silly people who can't mind their own business and have nothing better to do."

"Based on the fact that he won't talk to me, it only makes him look guilty."

Her gaze widened in surprise, but she quickly hid the emotion and placed her hands on her hips. "Get out," she said, pointing to the door. "Get out, and don't come back. We won't talk to you or any member of the media. The police will do their job and find out who committed such atrocious crimes. Until then, I suggest you watch yourself."

My heart skipped a beat and my stomach flipped. I narrowed my gaze at her, feeling like I had suddenly entered into battle with a gator. "Was that a threat?"

"Of course not," Cheryl said haughtily. "I'm just doing you a favor and telling you to not stick your nose where it doesn't belong. Sometimes if you do, it can get bitten off. But, I see you may have already done just that and someone has nibbled it."

I brought my hand to my nose and felt the scab across the bridge from the Filly Feed door. As I strode out, my body shook with fury, and maybe a little fear. The more distance I gained from the mayor's office, the more indignant I became. How dare they treat me like a piece of garbage on the street? And, the more I walked, the more convinced I was that Cheryl had indeed threatened me.

Who in the world did she think she was, tossing around insults and threats?

Wait until I told Byron. My conversation with the mayor and his wife had made them look guiltier than Satan himself.

9

WHEN I RETURNED to the office and told Harold what had happened, he whispered a few choice words under his breath and then leaned back in his chair with his hands laced on top of his head.

"Then we move to step two if they're going to pull that nonsense," he said.

"What's step two?"

"I don't know. Give me time."

Unsure if he meant a few minutes or a few days, I grabbed the mail that didn't belong to us and told him I'd be back later. Anger still simmered within me and I thought a walk would help burn it off.

Thankfully I didn't have any mail for Debbie, or I may just have caved and bought a donut. I delivered a letter to the vet, then one to the hardware store. On my way back to the office, I called Byron.

No answer, so I waited for the beep.

"Byron, it's Tilly. I just had an interesting meeting with the mayor and his wife. They're looking more and more guilty with each passing second. His wife, Cheryl... I think she threatened me. I'm pretty sure of it, but it wasn't an outright threat—more one that I had to read into. She's kind of aggressive, like an attack dog. Anyway, call me."

When I arrived at work, I noted Harold had locked up and disappeared. Probably went to the bank with his stack of ad money. After unlocking the door, I went inside and sat down behind my desk.

My phone rang again and I answered it without looking at the screen, figuring it was Byron.

"Hi, Tilly!" my mom sang over the line. "How's my girl?"

"Hi, Mama," I said. My shoulders sagged and homesickness washed over me. "I'm doing pretty good."

"Are you sure? I can tell by your voice—you're upset. Is it that awful man who left you? Is he back or some nonsense?"

"No," I said with a sigh. "I've been really busy."

As I told her everything, from the fireworks, to

me finding Mr. York, to my talk with the mayor, she listened intently.

When I finished, she clucked her tongue and said, "Oh my word. What has become of this world?"

"I don't know, Mama."

"What a tragedy, but it sounds like you're holding up."

"Yes."

"That's my girl. Remember you come from a line of tough women and you'll get through this."

"I know, Mama."

My mother's great-great-grandmother had helped slaves escape to the north before the Civil War, and Mama always reminded me of it when I was feeling down.

"Are the articles you're writing on the computer? Can I see them there, or trouble you to send them to me?"

"I'm not sure," I replied. "Harold had mentioned putting the paper online, but I don't know if he ever did."

"Find out. I can't wait to read your stuff."

"I will. Is Hank around?"

"Not right now. He's actually out back feeding Irwin some marshmallows."

My stepfather worked as a swamp tour guide for

tourists who wanted to see alligators. He'd adopted one gator and named him Irwin, after Steve Irwin, the Crocodile Hunter. Now of course gators and crocs were two different species, but when Steve had died, you would have thought my stepdad had lost his best friend. He had watched the show religiously and naming the gator after Mr. Irwin was his tribute to the fallen man.

"Okay, well, tell him I say hi."

"I will, baby. Hang in there. You're stronger than you think."

Even though forty lay just around the corner for me, the call with Mom had perked me up. Talking to her on the phone was like receiving a virtual hug, and it felt good.

I waited another half-hour for Harold, phoned him once and was sent to voicemail, and then decided to head back to my house. If he needed me, he could call.

As I drove the miles home, I tried to find some good music on the radio. I wasn't in the mood for country, I didn't need the stress that came with listening to talk radio, and I didn't like the music from my generation was now playing on the oldies station.

Sometimes, silence was golden.

When I pulled onto our road, I glanced at Mr. York's house. The police tape that had been across the driveway now lay on the ground and an SUV I didn't recognize sat outside the front door.

Was he being robbed?

I hurried inside my own home and dialed Byron again. The police definitely needed to check it out.

No answer.

For a long moment, I debated whether to call 9-1-1. What if it wasn't a robber, but some of his kin that had come?

The only way to find out was to march over there. Nerves tickled my belly as I recalled my conversation with the Ruperts: *I hope it isn't true that bad things happen in threes. I can't imagine what could be next.*

I hurried inside and grabbed the baseball bat Tommy had kept behind the door. On my way over to Mr. York's, I dialed 9-1-1 and explained that someone I didn't recognize had broken through the police tape and was at his house.

"I'll send someone, but it may be a while," the dispatcher said. "There was a rockslide between Oak Peak and Little River. They're all busy with that."

I hung up the phone and slid through the fence.

As I approached the SUV, my hands sweated, making my grip on the bat a little slick.

"Hello!" I yelled from just beyond the porch. "I've already called the police!"

I heard movement inside, but no one answered.

"They're going to be here any minute! You need to leave his things alone!"

As I readied my bat over my shoulder, a man appeared in the doorway behind the screen door.

Standing a little over six feet tall with a thin build, he smiled and waved, but I couldn't make out his facial features with the way the porch shadowed the doorway. "It's okay. My name's Derek. This is my dad's house."

Stunned, I could only stare at him as he stepped out and then I could get a good look at him.

Black hair, really friendly smile. Green or blue eyes—I wasn't sure which. Probably about my age. Yet, I couldn't recall Mr. York ever saying anything about a son, but then again, we weren't really close; just really neighborly.

"The cops are on their way," I said. "You better take a seat."

Derek nodded. "Sure. We can wait for them."

He stretched his long legs out in front of him as he sat down on the top step. "Pretty day, isn't it?"

I relaxed just a little. He seemed harmless enough, but that didn't mean I trusted him.

"Do you live over there?" he asked, pointing to my house.

How stupid did he think I was? "That's really none of your business."

"Fair enough."

We sat in silence as I kept my eye on him and he glanced around the yard, his gaze settling behind me where the shed had been. "I'm guessing that's where the fireworks were kept. Looks pretty burnt up."

I didn't look over my shoulder in case he tried to lunge at me. I still had my bat at the ready.

"It's too bad about that orchard," he continued. "I bet it was pretty when the trees were in bloom."

In the distance, I heard a siren and sighed in relief. The police would be able to figure out if this guy was who he said.

A few moments later, a police car rolled into the driveway and came to a stop. Byron got out and hurried over to me.

"What are you doing, Tilly?" he asked.

"I saw this guy in Mr. York's house and figured I better call. He says he's his son, but I doubt it. Mr. York never said he had any kids."

Byron rolled his eyes at me and then approached

Derek. "I'm sorry about this, sir. Tilly here lives in the house over there. She's the one who found your father."

Derek stood, his gaze boring into me. A blush crept up my neck and into my cheeks as he strolled over.

"I'm sorry you had to go through that," he said, his voice soft. "I truly am Derek York, Tilly."

Jeez, he had the prettiest eyes. One moment they looked green, then he turned his head just a bit, and they became blue. How did that happen?

"Byron!" I called as I shifted my weight from one foot to the other. Being under Derek's stare filled me with uneasiness.

"He was down at the station earlier today, Tilly," Byron said, coming back over to me. "We verified his identification. Put down the damn bat."

I lowered my weapon to my side while Byron grabbed my arm. "Excuse us, Derek. We'll be right back."

He pulled me about ten feet away and didn't release me. "What's gotten into you?" he hissed. "You're leaving me all these crazy messages about who you think committed the murder and now you're threatening Mr. York's son with a baseball bat?"

"My messages aren't crazy! They're based on facts and every single theory I've given you makes perfect sense."

Byron shook his head. "You're going off gossip and an overactive imagination. Let us do our jobs. Please?"

"Fine," I said, hefting the bat over my shoulder again. "I won't contact you again."

"I didn't say that. I want you to—"

"It's fine, Byron. I won't call you about the murder or the fireworks any longer."

He stared at me for a long second then sighed. "All right. I'm going to leave. How are the chickens doing?"

I ground my jaw as I debated how to answer. Byron had gotten my hackles up again by dismissing my perfectly good theories, and I wasn't sure who had made me madder: him or the mayor.

"They're delicious."

"What?"

"I said, they're delicious," I called over my shoulder. "Bye, Byron!"

A deep feeling of satisfaction rolled through me and a smile turned my lips when I heard him gasp. He had no idea if I had been serious or not.

I once again approached Derek.

"You two seem to know each other well," he murmured, crossing his arms over his chest.

"Not really," I replied, having no intention of getting into my dating history. "I'm sorry about your dad. He was a good guy. He never mentioned you, though."

Derek nodded as he glanced around the yard. "We had our differences. I had some problems when I was younger and I don't think he ever forgave me for the rough time I put him and Mom through. We weren't close, especially after Mom died."

My manners didn't allow me to question what the 'rough time' had entailed, but boy, did I wonder.

"What are you going to do with the house?"

"Dad left it to me," he replied with a shrug, "but I'm not sure what to do with it. I guess I may be your new neighbor."

I blushed as Mr. Tall, Dark, and Oh-So Handsome grinned. But then a sinking feeling hit my stomach.

"Haven't quite decided though," he continued. "A lot of memories here for me. I may just sell it, but we'll see. Right now, I'm going through his stuff."

As I listened, I realized I had another suspect in Mr. York's murder standing right in front of me.

He and his dad weren't close. What if Derek's

troubled youth had spilled over into a troubled adulthood? What if those troubles required a great deal of money?

Derek would know his father had made a small fortune when he sold off the land, and he'd just inherited himself a nice house... money was always a perfect motive for murder.

10

My other best friend besides Debbie was named Carla and lived in Cedarville. She'd been away on a cruise to Mexico with her husband, Mac, for the past two weeks. I was glad that they finally got their honeymoon after five years of marriage and saving every penny they could, but I had missed her terribly. When she called the next day, I might as well have won a million dollars I was so excited.

"Tilly!"

"Carla! Oh, my goodness. How was your trip? Tell me everything!"

"Come over later today," she said with a laugh. "I'll show you the pictures and tell you all about it."

We agreed to meet at her house around two,

which worked out perfect for me. I spent some time at the office and then told Harold I'd be taking the rest of the afternoon off. We'd decided I would interview Derek York for the article and obituary on his father, and he had generously agreed to do that the next day. Harold was knee deep in counting the ad money rolling in, and we still hadn't secured an interview with the police.

"Have a great weekend," the man said as he tinkered with ad placement on the computer. "Make sure to have the article on York to me on Monday morning."

"Will do."

My excitement grew as I drove to Cedarville. When I arrived at her small white home with green trim, I jumped out of my truck and ran to the door. She flung it open and we embraced. Her hug felt almost as good as the phone call from my mom.

"Tilly, I've been reading the papers and the gossip tree is on fire," she exclaimed. "What on Earth has happened while we've been gone? What did you do to your head and nose?"

I pulled away and studied her. With an African American grandmother, Carla's skin had always been tawny. After the cruise, she had a beautiful tan.

Her curls hung to her shoulders and her brown eyes gleamed with concern, but she looked rested and relaxed.

"It's been pretty crazy around here. I hit my head on my nightstand and cracked my nose against a door."

She burst out laughing and I couldn't help but grin. I really did have a knack for self-injury.

"At least that hasn't changed about you. Come in and tell me everything," she said as she grabbed my hand and pulled me into the kitchen. "I made coffee."

I sat at the table and glanced around the familiar kitchen. The grass-green walls and white cabinets reminded me of spring. Her house had become my second home, or maybe my third since I spent so much time at Debbie's Deliciousness.

After Tommy left, I'd found out that she and Mac hadn't liked him all that much. I wish they'd had said something, but I probably wouldn't have listened. As far as I was concerned, our marriage had been going great. In fact, if she had mentioned her dislike for him, it might have driven a wedge in our friendship.

Carla brought me a cup along with some cream

and sugar. I stuck to my good choices and only had the cream.

"Was your property hurt?" Carla asked. "Are Tinker and Belle okay? Tell me about the fire."

I told her everything in great detail from the moment the fireworks had woken me up, to Tinker throwing up and having accidents all over my bedroom, to finding Mr. York's body.

"While he lay dying, he did tell me that the person who lit the fireworks and the one who had stabbed him were one and the same."

"Goodness," Carla said, shaking her head. "What a horrible thing."

"I have a few ideas on who's responsible, but Byron told me yesterday to mind my own business."

"Matilda Elizabeth Donner, are you trying to solve the crimes?"

"Of course not. I'll leave that to the professionals. I'm simply passing on some theories."

"I feel like you're sticking your nose where it doesn't belong."

"I'm really not. I'm just giving him information I'm getting from doing my interviews. That's it."

Carla nodded as she furrowed her brow and rested her chin in her palm and her elbow on the table. "It's interesting. I mean, you have to look at who's going to benefit the most. That's going to lead you to the murderer."

Carla loved reading mystery novels and rarely missed the crime shows on television. She probably knew more about investigating a murder than Byron or Sheriff Connor.

"Well, the mayor definitely benefitted because the fireworks are gone, and everyone thinks Mr. York did it."

"Except Mr. York told you he didn't. It's easy to blame the dead, and I'd believe him over a politician."

"Then there's Minnie," I said after taking a sip of coffee. "She knew the fireworks were there and had a beef with Mr. York about her cows being on his land. No pun intended. She could have wanted to get him in trouble."

Carla laughed at my bad joke.

"She'd have to be crazy to do something like that," she said. "Wouldn't she?"

"Oh, I think she's a little cuckoo, Carla. That woman is obsessed with those cows. I've never seen anything like it."

"Even with your stepdad and that gator? Irwin?"

I frowned, realizing my stepdad's infatuation with the gator did resemble Minnie's feelings about her cows. "Maybe Hank isn't firing on all cylinders, either."

"Well, I suppose if we're going to factor a bit of crazy into the equation, then Minnie qualifies as a suspect."

"Agreed."

"Who else benefits?"

I debated on whether to tell her about York's son, but I wasn't sure why. Maybe because he was the first man who had caught my attention since Tommy and he also had a motive for murder.

"Mr. York has a son," I finally blurted out. "He inherited his daddy's house."

Carla arched an eyebrow. "Now, that's interesting. Do you know how much the house is worth?"

I shook my head. "Before we moved in, Mr. York used to own all the land. Mine, Minnie's and the Ruperts'. He cut it up and sold it off, then retired. My guess is he made a really nice chunk of change from it."

"What's his name? The son?"

"Derek."

"Do you think there's more for him to inherit besides the property? Some bank accounts and stuff like that?"

"I'm sure it's a possibility. I don't know anything

about his finances. I didn't even know his first name. I always called him Mr. York."

"Hmm... even with just the house, it's definitely a motive for murder."

"That's what I thought."

I *really* didn't want Derek to be guilty, so I hated to even throw his name into the pot of potential suspects.

"I never knew Mr. York had any kids," I said, unable to meet her gaze as my cheeks heated.

"Have you met him?"

"Yes."

"And?"

I sighed and rolled my eyes. "And I threatened to beat him with a baseball bat because I thought he was robbing Mr. York's house."

Carla threw her head back and laughed until tears ran down her cheeks. As she gasped for breath, she said, "That seems perfectly logical to me, Tilly."

A giggle escaped me and after a few seconds, we were both in tears again. The tension and worry from the past few days seemed to ooze out of me, and it felt really good.

"So what's he like?" Carla asked as she wiped her face with her fingertips.

"He's super cute," I replied. "But I didn't talk to him much."

"Why not?"

"Well, first I was embarrassed that I'd confronted him with a baseball bat over my shoulder. Second, Byron was there telling me what an idiot I was. It just seemed best to remove myself from the situation."

"What does he look like?"

An image of Derek popped into my mind and my cheeks heated once again as I squirmed in my seat. "Black hair. Tall. Green or blue eyes... I'm not sure."

"He sounds cuter than a bunny butt."

"You're right," I said with a sigh. "He's really nice to look at. He also told me that he had some problems in his childhood but didn't specify what they were. What if those problems carried on into adulthood, who's to say he's not desperate for money?"

"Desperate people do desperate things," Carla murmured.

"Yes, they do."

"What's he doing with the house?"

"He said he's thinking about moving in."

Carla sat back and grinned as she ran her finger along the rim of her coffee cup. "How exciting for you, Ms. Single-and-Needing-a-Date."

"Pfft," I replied. "I don't need a date. I don't need anyone but Tinker and Belle. Did I tell you I think Tinker is in love with a chicken?"

It was a good time to change the subject. I had Carla laughing again as I explained Tinker's obsession.

"Wait!" she yelled. "When did you get chickens?"

"When Byron brought them to me as a gift!"

Carla hung her head and rubbed the bridge of her nose as she giggled. "What type of man brings a woman he wants to date chickens?"

"I don't know. I'm sure there are some women who would appreciate it, but the gesture only solidifies that I don't belong with him."

"You're right," Carla replied. "Chickens are not the way to your heart."

Well, maybe they were... if they were fried, covered in batter, and served with a side of ranch.

"Who gave you chickens, Tilly?" Carla's husband, Mac, asked as he came into the kitchen from the laundry room, his mega-watt smile gleaming. I'd always liked him and appreciated how he always gave Carla and me our space. Also, I'd often wondered how he got his teeth to be so white.

"Byron."

He shook his head and came around the table. I

stood and he gave me a quick hug. "You don't belong with him. Good call. I'll leave you two ladies to keep gossiping."

As Mac strode through the house and bounded up the stairs, I noted the love in Carla's gaze as she watched him.

Deep down, I wanted someone besides Tinker and Belle to look at me the way Carla did at Mac. I wanted to feel loved and cherished. Sometimes, when I was with the two, my chest seemed empty— just a large, dark void waiting to be filled.

"Let me see some pictures of your vacation," I said.

For the next hour, we sat shoulder to shoulder as she went through her phone and I received a detailed description of every picture. Beaches, palm trees, fruity drinks, smiles, blue water... maybe one day I'd be able to treat myself to such an extravaganza.

"I better get going," I said, as I stood and stretched my arms over my head.

"It was good to see you. I'll talk to you soon."

We hugged before I crawled back into my truck and sped off, my mood drastically improved. For a little while, I was able to forget about the murder and mayhem that had taken over my life.

Hopefully, there would be an arrest soon, but in my view, the list of suspects seemed to keep growing and that bothered me. Mr. York had been a nice man, and I didn't like it when bad things happened to nice people.

I just wanted the perpetrator caught so I'd feel safe.

11

THE NEXT DAY, I paced my kitchen nervously as I waited for Derek to show. I'd scrubbed my counters clean, scooped out Belle's litterbox, and prayed the odor from Tinker's accidents had fully disappeared. But I kept wondering, why in the world was I trying to impress Derek?

A knock sounded promptly at eleven. With sweaty palms, I opened the door to find him carrying a bouquet of flowers.

"These are for you," he said with a grin as he extended them to me.

"What for?" I asked, shocked, horrified and pleased all at once.

"To show that I'm not a robber and really a nice guy."

The room suddenly became very warm as Tinker and Belle loped in to check out our guest.

"Come in," I replied, not meeting his gaze and suddenly feeling very shy. "They're very pretty. Thank you."

After my terrible divorce, I appreciated a man treating me so sweetly. As I filled a vase with water, I stared at the bouquet with a few tears in my eyes. Daisies, baby's breath, and a couple of blue roses.

I had to admit, I appreciated them much more than I had the chickens. Derek stood patiently while Tinker and Belle sniffed him. After a few minutes, Belle trotted off and Tinker lay under the table.

"What happened to the dog's nose?" he asked. "She's got little scratches and cuts on it."

"That's Tinker, and I think she's in love with a chicken or two," I said with a sigh. "She lays there all day by the pen and lets them thump on her snout. I'm not sure what to do about it."

Derek chuckled and shook his head. "I guess we can't control who we love."

"I guess not," I murmured, still unable to meet his gaze. What was it about this man that made my insides feel all wonky? "Have a seat. And thank you for the flowers. That was really nice of you."

I moved around the counter and sat across from

him. As he grinned at me, I couldn't imagine him being a murderer, but then people said the same thing about Ted Bundy.

"Can you tell me a bit about your dad?"

"He was a good man," Derek began. "I remember a lot from when I was young. We used to play catch right here where this house is now. He used to take me fishing up by Little River.

There was a lot of laughter in our house. He always wanted to help others."

"And he knew the late Mayor Shelton, correct?" I asked.

"Yes. They were good friends. I remember thinking how cool I was because he drank beer with the town mayor right on our porch during the summer months."

We both laughed, and I remember thinking how cool *I* was because my stepdad made friends with gators.

"Did you get along with the current mayor, Doug Shelton, when you were young? Were you friends with him?"

Derek shook his head. "He was a bully if I remember right. Not a very nice guy."

Some people just don't change.

"But your dad agreed to help him by storing the fireworks."

"That's what I've heard, but I wasn't sure if it was true or not. It does make sense, though. Like I said, he always wanted to help others."

His eyes appeared green in my kitchen and the longer he stared at me, the hotter the room became.

"Do you want some water?" I asked, abruptly getting to my feet.

"Sure."

I busied myself getting us each a glass and filling it, then returned to the table.

"You said you and your dad weren't close."

"No. Not when he died."

"Why?"

As I sat back down, I felt his stare on me again. I could only drink water and fiddle with my pen for so long before I had to meet his gaze.

"Are you asking for the paper?"

"This is off the record," I replied. "I'm just trying to get a grasp of your relationship with him."

Actually, I was really curious. Derek seemed normal, but he'd fully admitted he had skeletons rattling around in his closet. I wanted to know what they were.

Maybe Carla was right and I tended to stick my nose in places it didn't belong.

"I developed a drug problem in high school," he said, his voice quiet and laced with regret. "I stole from my parents, worried my mom sick, and really angered my dad. After I moved out, I'd come back and break into their house when they weren't home to take anything I could get my hands on to sell so I could get my fix. I finally got clean about ten years ago, but the damage had been done. My dad blamed me for my mom's death. She had a heart attack right after they'd sent me back to rehab for the fourth time. He told me the stress I caused her killed her."

I bit my bottom lip as I took notes. "I'm sorry to hear that. That's quite the guilt trip to deal with."

"It was actually my mom dying and my dad blaming me that finally got me sober. It was a hard bullet to take and a difficult thing to live with."

My knowledge of drugs was limited to over-the-counter pain relievers, so I didn't have anything deep or meaningful to say. I just found the whole story incredibly sad.

"What did you do to your forehead and nose?" he asked.

The change in the conversation startled me. I

brought my finger to my offended spot and felt the scab. I really didn't want to explain it all again.

"Let's just say I'm a little accident prone."

His smile widened and caused my heart to flutter. Jeez, he was cute.

We stared at each other a few moments as I attempted to decide if he had murdered his own father. I leaned on the side of no, but did I really think that, or just wish it?

"Is there anything else?" he asked. "I've got to sign some papers down at the bank."

I found that odd because the bank closed at ten on Saturdays. I glanced over at the clock above my oven and it was nearly noon.

Maybe he just didn't want to continue the conversation?

"The bank manager asked me to come in today," he explained, as if he'd read my mind. "He said he wanted me to sign with some privacy."

"What about the obituary? Do you have anything to add to that?"

Derek sighed and ran a hand through his hair. "Honestly, Tilly, I spoke to him maybe three times a year. His birthday, my birthday, and Christmas. He never invited me here. I gave up inviting him for holidays about five years ago."

"Where did you live?" I asked, wondering if Mr. York would have had to travel far.

"Two hours south of here."

Nope. Not far at all.

"What about a service?" I asked. "When's that?"

"He didn't want one. His will is very cut and dry. He wanted to be cremated and I'm to spread his ashes along with my mom's in the mountains."

"He kept your mom's ashes all this time?"

"Yes, he did. I find it a little disturbing that they've been sitting in the closet for ten years."

I nodded, unsure how I felt about not having a burial. A funeral, or some type of service, always seemed like a nice way for people to say their final goodbyes. "Well, I guess we can put that in the obituary."

"I know you've been tasked with writing an article about him, but I have no idea about his life. For the past twenty years, we haven't had a relationship. He was a good dad until I got screwed up. There's some stuff at the house that I can go through and put something together for you. I know he served in the military before he met my mom. Things like that."

"That sounds good. I'd appreciate your help. Thank you."

As I walked him to the door, I began to think that if he could take care of the past, maybe I could fill in the blanks about the present.

I thanked him again for the flowers and waved as he walked across my yard, slid through the fence, and headed to his potential new home.

Was he guilty of murder?

It really didn't seem like it to me.

Pushing the thoughts aside, I went about my chores. While cleaning the chicken coop, I noted the hens were a little distant, but at least they weren't attacking me. I mowed the spot of grass Minnie's cows hadn't chewed on, then picked up dog poo. The remnants of the nectarine orchard still reminded me of an evil forest, and I wondered what would become of the land. I missed the sweet smell of the trees in bloom. Sometimes it became almost overwhelming, but then the wind would shift and the odor of Minnie's cows smacked me in the face. Now, the air was filled with the scent of burnt wood, and it saddened me.

Would the Ruperts raze the trees and plant new ones? I certainly hoped so. I had the evil forest in back of me and a potential murderer living next door. If I didn't get a hold of my imagination, I'd end up locking myself in the closet with my baseball bat.

I went inside and folded some laundry. After the chores had been completed, I sat down at the table and looked over my meager notes. It made me nervous that I could be living next to a killer. I placed my face in my palms and shut my eyes. My nerves had already been frayed with the fire and Mr. York's death, and now with Derek moving in... well, I just didn't know what to think.

Tinker placed her head in my lap and I stroked her golden brow. She always knew when I needed some love.

"You have to let me know if someone shows up who doesn't belong here," I said. "You don't have to do anything about it, but just let me know."

She tilted her head and lifted her ears as if unsure of her assigned job. Then she trotted over to her dog door and went outside. I glanced out the window to see her heading for the chicken coop again.

Belle strutted in and jumped into my lap. I stroked her silky black fur absently as I watched Tinker lay down and shove her nose through the chicken wire.

"So much for her being my watchdog," I mumbled to Belle. "That dog is infatuated with those chickens."

The quiet settled around me and I considered stretching out on the couch and taking a nap. Or, I could go for a walk. What I really needed to do was get the article on Mr. York written, and I began to think that it and the obituary should be blended in one piece.

The phone ringing startled me so much, I jumped out of my chair, sending Belle scrambling. She hissed and gave me the side-eye as I tried to catch my breath.

"Hello?" I answered after the third ring.

"Tilly, it's Debbie."

Her low tone surprised me further. "What's going on? Are you okay?"

"Yes. I've got a couple of customers out front and I don't want them to hear me."

"Okay..."

"Barb at the bank just called me, and you're never going to believe this."

"What?" I asked softly, and immediately felt silly. No one was around on my end to hear this secret.

"She was there when York's boy went in to sign some papers. Guess how much Derek inherited?"

My heart thundered in my chest. Leave it to Debbie to find out the actual numbers.

"How much?"

"Not only did he get the house, but he received just over a million dollars," she whispered.

My breath caught in my throat as I tried to wrap my mind around the number. I felt secure when I had a thousand saved up in my bank account. I couldn't even imagine what sitting on a stack of money that high would feel like.

"If that's not a motive for murder, I don't know what is," Debbie said. "Well, now we've got another suspect, and I think this one looks the best, don't you?"

I had to admit, she had a point.

A million dollars was a great motive for murder.

12

SUNDAY CAME and went with such speed, it almost gave me whiplash. Derek had stopped by as promised with a box of stuff, but I hadn't answered the door. He knew I was home because my truck sat in the driveway, but I'd huddled under my bedroom window while Tinker barked at him. Handsome, yes. A murderer, maybe. Out of all the theories Debbie and I had concocted, he seemed to be the one who benefited the most, and that's what I had to look for, according to Carla.

I arrived at the office early Monday a little cranky and very tired. Nightmares of my potentially homicidal neighbor plagued me, and my mood only worsened when I sifted through the mail. More stuff that wasn't ours which reminded me that I hadn't gotten my personal mail at home in three or four days. I imagined it was the same there.

"Nice piece on York," Harold said when he walked in.

"Thank you."

"Something wrong, Tilly?" he asked as he sat behind his desk.

"No. Just tired of thinking about who killed him."

"That's not really your job, is it? Your job is to *report* on the goings-on around town, not to *investigate* the who, when, where or why of someone's death."

I nodded, knowing full well he was correct. Yet, I couldn't stop running over the theories and giving myself nightmares.

"So maybe you should stop trying to solve a crime that isn't yours to solve," Harold said.

"I'm sure you're right."

"On the flip-side, Tilly, things are going so well here at the paper, I'm going to give you a raise on your next paycheck. You're doing an amazing job and all this ad money wouldn't be rolling in without your hard work."

A blush crawled up my neck and over my cheeks. "Thank you, Harold. I appreciate that."

"Your face looks a little thinner," he said, narrowing his gaze on me. "Are you losing weight?"

The off-topic question brought a smile as I tried to hide my excitement. Losing weight and a raise? Maybe this day wasn't so bad. "Really?"

"I don't know if you're tired or you're dropping some pounds, but yes, your face looks thinner."

I pinched my palm as my grin widened and my mood improved drastically. "Thank you for the raise, and the compliment, Harold. If it's okay, I'll be back in a bit. I have an appointment."

He nodded and returned his attention to his computer.

I walked out of the office and headed to Debbie's with a little bounce in my step. Harold didn't need to know I was meeting her and Carla for coffee.

"Tilly!" Debbie exclaimed as I walked into the bakery.

"Hi."

"Oh, my. What's going on? You look exhausted."

"Nothing," I said with a sigh. "I'm tired of thinking about who committed murder and why. I'm not sleeping well."

"Let's sit down. Any donuts today?"

"No, thanks." I grabbed a table in the corner while Debbie poured us both coffee.

"Tell me what's going on," she said, reaching across the table and squeezing my fingers.

"It's all I can think about. Who lit those fireworks and murdered Mr. York? It's driving me crazy!"

"Completely understandable. It's an insane time in this town."

"It's not even my job to solve the case. I'm just supposed to report on it."

Debbie glanced around at the few customers, then leaned in across the table. "Do you really think Byron is capable of solving the crime?"

"Of course he is," I replied. "He's the police."

Debbie arched an eyebrow at me and I sighed. Without saying it, she revealed she didn't have much faith in Byron, but I hoped his boss would come through and find the murderer. I didn't like hiding in my bedroom every time someone knocked on the door.

We each took a sip of our coffee, then Debbie leaned over. "How's your new, very rich neighbor?"

"You mean the one who could be a killer?"

Just then the door chimed and Carla walked in. Debbie stood and gave her a hug and asked a million questions about her trip before getting her a cup of coffee. As Carla sat down, Debbie waited on a couple of customers, then joined us once again.

"Did you hear about Tilly's neighbor?" she asked.

Carla nodded as I rolled my eyes. "The gossip vine is lit up like a Christmas tree. I also heard that there are a lot of women in the Tri-Town area who are looking to score themselves a millionaire boyfriend. That man is about to get overrun with willing women."

"That's just dumb," I said. "You'd think they'd wait until they knew whether he was guilty of killing his father or not."

"Speaking of guilty," Debbie said under her breath as she stood. "One of our suspects just walked in."

I turned and glanced over my shoulder to see the mayor strutting toward the counter, a large smile on his face while he greeted a few people. With us being tucked away in a corner, he didn't see us, but my anger rose once again at the memory of the dismissal in his office. I worked for the paper and I was going to get to the bottom of the fireworks scandal, no matter what it took. There was too much town history involved for me to ignore it. He'd defied the law, and I wanted to hear why directly from him.

After taking a deep breath and straightening my

blouse, I tucked a lock of hair behind my ear and marched over to the counter.

"Excuse me, Mayor," I said as I tapped him on the shoulder. "I don't know if you remember me, but I'm Tilly from the Tri-Town Times. You and I had an—"

"Of course I remember you," he said, his smile still in place yet his gaze darting around the store.

"Oh, good," I replied, realizing he had become a different man from the one I had met in his office now that we were in the public arena. "I was wondering if I could steal a few moments of your time and discuss the illegal fireworks on Mr. York's land."

His smile began to falter and he sighed.

"I think it's a wonderful idea, Mayor Shelton," Debbie said with a grin as she handed him his coffee and donut. "A lot of us don't understand your thinking of wanting to bring back the Fourth of July celebration, especially after it decimated our town. We'd love to hear your side of it, and what better way to do it than with the friendly reporter from the paper?"

He shot Debbie a glare while she batted her eyelashes at him. After grabbing his coffee, he nodded and I motioned him to an empty table where we could talk. My nervousness from days ago was nowhere to be found. Instead, I wanted answers. Was I living next door to a killer? Was Minnie crazy enough about her cows to kill her neighbor over them? Did the mayor of my small town have a murderous heart?

Mayor Shelton stared at me expectantly over his coffee cup as his leg shook under the table.

I found it almost laughable that I seemed to be making him nervous. Either that or he didn't need any more coffee for the day.

"Mr. York told me the fireworks were yours," I began. "Can you tell me why you brought them into our town when they've been outlawed? By your own father?"

"Yes," he said and set down his cup. "I'll be happy to."

I noted his voice had softened and he grinned at me as if I were his best friend. Quite the change from the bombastic and challenging man I'd encountered in his office.

"When I was young, the Fourth of July celebration was something everyone looked forward to," he said. "The stores along Oak Avenue would all decorate their windows and doors in red, white and blue. People spent days in the kitchen preparing for the town potluck. It was all anyone could talk about from the middle of June up until the big day. My mother and I used to make a homemade calendar that counted down until the big party. My friends used to come over to look at it and we'd get so excited.

"Then, on July 4th, we'd all gather at Oak Park, which used to be located where the city hall is now. All the families together, the kids running around, people sharing their food, blankets spread out... It was a magical day in Oak Peak, and I remember the feeling of community."

"It sounds nice," I said. The way he described the event reminded me of a scene from a small-town movie—picturesque and happy.

"Then when the sun went down, the volunteer fire department lit the fireworks. The sky exploded in color and the crowds went wild. It would be the talk of the town for days afterward."

"Except for that year," I said. "When the town burned to the ground."

The mayor nodded and sighed. "Yes. Except that year."

"If the fire department was in charge of the fireworks, how did the fire happen?"

"I honestly don't know. I remember my heart

thumping when one of the trees caught fire. That quickly jumped to a building. We were so dang dry that year from the drought, everything was like a tinderbox. My mama grabbed my hand and we ran from the park to our house. So much pushing and shoving... that community feeling had been taken over by the desperation of every man for himself. Fear drove every decision from then on."

I could understand that. I'd been scared to death as I watched the orchard fire creep closer to my home.

"My dad decided to get rid of the celebration. He didn't even rebuild the park. Instead, he erected the city hall in its place, as if he could pave over the good times and memories of what that park represented."

The mayor stared wistfully into space, as if our discussion had brought him back to a better time in his life.

"So, I want to recreate that," he said. "I want to bring back that feeling of community and joy that we all experienced on the Fourth of July."

Maybe he should have started by having a town potluck and gently eased into the idea of fireworks.

"These days, the holiday comes and goes," he said with a sigh. "It's the birth of our great country and should be celebrated. It's just another day in our little town, while being so much more."

That may be the case, but people had issues with the day. Some had lost their livelihood. Some had lost their homes. It wasn't the greatest day for everyone.

"Why did you ask Mr. York to hide the fireworks?"

He huffed and crossed his arms over his chest. "Because he lived way out there. He didn't have many neighbors. There's no one to snoop into his business."

"I'm one of his neighbors," I said. "I'm the one who found him right before he died."

The mayor's face paled and his eyes widened. "I'm sorry. I didn't know that."

I nodded and jotted down some notes, then met his gaze again. "You were getting some flak from your secret committee on bringing back the celebration, right?"

"I don't know if I'd call it a secret committee."

"Well, there were only six people asked to be on it, right?"

"Yes."

"And no one else knew about it, correct?"

"I don't know. I guess so."

"Did you tell those you invited to the committee not to say anything to anyone else in town?"

"I don't recall," he replied as his cheeks reddened.

"Well, if all that's true," I snapped, "then I'd say it was a secret."

I wrote more in my notebook and I could feel his angry stare on me. Too bad. I was now determined to get to the bottom of the fireworks issue and the murder and pass my findings on to the police so they could make an arrest. I was tired of living in fear and questioning everyone's motives.

"Here's my theory," I said. "I think you got some feedback from your little committee and they told you your idea was a horrible one, but you already had the fireworks. You needed to destroy them. Maybe lighting them was an accident. Maybe it was intentional. I don't know. However, you didn't want the situation to get out of hand and you certainly didn't want to be blamed for any of it. You told Mr. York you wouldn't take the heat and you asked him to. He said—"

The mayor stood so abruptly, his chair toppled to the floor behind him. "I won't have this pinned on me," he hissed as he fisted his hands at his sides.

"Don't you *dare* try to do that. I'll ruin your boss and that rag he owns."

I stared at his back as he stomped to the door and out into the street, my heart pounding so quickly, I thought I may pass out. He certainly hadn't liked what I had to say.

"Looks like you got his briefs in a bunch," Carla said, laying her hand on my shoulder. "With the election coming up, he doesn't want the bad press."

I nodded and squeezed her fingers, understanding that bad press could ruin his chances at re-election.

But, if he were a murderer, he shouldn't be in office—he should be behind bars.

13

I RETURNED to the office and wrote my piece on the mayor while it was still fresh in my mind. With great effort, I kept my own theories out of the article and instead focused on what the mayor had wanted to do for the town, what his good intentions had been. Don't get me wrong, I wanted to be very critical to him, but I had also heard his threat loud and clear. I'd write facts, not my own conjecture.

Besides, Harold would never allow a hatchet job.

After I turned in the article, I glanced at the clock and saw it was time for me to head home.

"Here's your paycheck, Tilly," Harold said, handing me an envelope. "Don't spend it all in one place."

"Thanks. I'll see you in the morning."

He waved as I walked out to my truck. After sliding in, I opened the envelope and gasped at the amount. It was far more than I had expected, so I decided I'd buy myself something nice, then put the rest away for an emergency or a time when I wasn't working. Or maybe it would be my first deposit toward that cruise I wanted to take. So many options. I glanced at my phone and realized I had a message.

My stomach curled when I heard my ex-husband Tommy's voice. I closed my eyes and pinched the bridge of my nose as I tried to make out the garbled sounds. He'd most likely been driving in or around Little River. Reception was terrible up north.

I heard something about him possibly stopping by, but the rest was indecipherable. I debated whether to call him back or not, and decided I should. He never phoned to say hello, so it must be important.

"Tilly?" he answered on the second ring. "Did you get my message?"

"Yes, but I couldn't understand a word of it."

"Sorry about that. I was driving from Little River to Oak Peak. Reception is bad."

"I know, Tommy," I said with a sigh. "What do you want?"

"Well, I'm still paying the insurance on your house, Tilly. I'd really appreciate it if you could get a policy of your own so I can cancel mine."

Tommy had felt so awful about leaving me, he'd given me the house and had apparently been paying the insurance, as well. I truly had no idea.

"I'll make some calls when I get home," I said.

"I've got a kid to feed and another one on the way. If you could take care of that soon, I'd appreciate it."

I rolled my eyes and grimaced. How nice of him to throw that in my face. "Is there anything else?"

"No. I'm just heading back to Little River, so I'm sure I'll cut out soon. Are you okay, Tilly?"

The concern in his voice saddened me. I had thought we would be together forever, and sometimes I still missed him. I didn't want to discuss my life, or his.

"I'm fine, Tommy. Thanks. I'll get the insurance figured out."

Not wanting to talk to him anymore, I hung up. Today had been great: a fat paycheck, I was losing weight, according to Harold, and I'd interviewed the mayor. I didn't need my past creeping in and bringing me down.

I turned on the radio and sang a country song

about lost love at the top of my lungs as I drove home with the windows rolled down. My hair lashed me in the face and my throat ached while recalling the pain Tommy had caused me, how he'd shattered my dreams of the future.

"You really need to put it behind you," I said aloud as I drove by Derek's. "Feeling sorry for what could have been is not going to make anything better."

Derek stood at the back fence watching Betty Frank from the feed store unload bales of hay from the bed of a pickup truck. She dug her hooks into them, then tossed them to Minnie, who carried and stacked them inside the barn while Tulip and Sunflower stared at them over the fence. Both women were so strong, and I wondered if they did pullups in Minnie's barn together. Derek waved at them and Minnie wiped her brow and walked across the pasture to meet him.

How cozy.

I pulled into my driveway, parked, and exited the truck. Tinker ran toward me from the side of the house, where she probably visited her chickens.

"Hey, girl!" I called as she came at me like a freight train. "I'm glad to see you, too!"

She jumped at me, almost sending me to the

ground. Thankfully, I caught myself before I fell. I hugged and kissed her while rubbing her body, her happiness at seeing me soothing the pain the phone call had caused.

"Let's go inside," I said while I rounded the bumper of the truck.

A gasp escaped me when I realized my front door hung open.

"What the heck, Tinker?" I whispered.

In my exhaustion this morning, had I forgotten to lock it? Maybe a breeze had come through and blown it open?

I glanced down at Tinker who stared up at me adoringly. She didn't seem too concerned. I had to believe that if someone were in my house, she'd let me know.

Should I call the police? It seemed like the smart thing to do, but what if it was a case of me being absentminded? Then I'd feel foolish. But maybe it was best to be safe and embarrassed than confront someone in my house and be sorry.

Who could it be? Derek? The mayor I had angered so badly earlier in the day? Maybe Minnie, making sure I didn't have any evidence of her crime? Tommy had been in town... perhaps he'd come by and never closed the door? It wouldn't have been the first time. The man had often acted like he'd been born in a barn and hardly ever closed doors. It had been a strange habit for me to accept. Besides, I never got around to changing the locks after he left.

I pulled out my phone as Tinker trotted into the house without a worry. A moment later, she stood in the doorway and wagged her tail. Her behavior indicated that if there had been any danger, it was now gone.

After I dialed 9-1-1, I held my thumb over the send button and quietly crept up the stairs and into the house wishing I had brought down the baseball bat I'd slept with the previous night. It still lay on the floor next to my bed. Glancing around, I didn't notice anything out of place in the kitchen or living room. As I crept upstairs to the bedrooms, my hands began to shake and sweat. Tinker ran up in front of me and waited on the landing, her tail still wagging. I checked my bedroom, then the two others. Again, everything looked normal. I exhaled a long breath and trotted back downstairs, certain that either I or Tommy had left the door open. Besides putting the insurance in my name, I really needed to change the locks. He still had some stuff in the house that I'd moved to one of the empty bedrooms, but that didn't mean he could come and go as he pleased. This would definitely need to stop.

I went out to feed the chickens with Tinker. They once again tried to peck my legs, but at least they weren't quite as vicious about it. Maybe we'd get along at some point.

When I returned to the house, I fed Tinker, then set down food for Belle.

"Come eat, Belly-Belle!"

There wasn't a response and I worried she'd slipped out, although she'd never done that before. As a true couch diva, she preferred to watch the world go by from the comfort of her home than to get her feet dirty. I imagined her curled up in a windowsill somewhere catching the last of the day's summer rays.

I made myself a grilled cheese sandwich and turned on the television. Tinker stretched out at my feet and soon snored quietly. Judge Judy dressed down the defendant, but I didn't hear much of it because I couldn't stop turning the York case over and over in my mind.

If I looked at who benefitted from it, the list was long. Of course, there was Derek, who could now call himself a millionaire. Heck, if I went by that measure, Harold had profited from the murder, and so had I. Ad revenue had gone through the roof, and I had a big, fat paycheck to put in the bank. It would remain to be seen if the mayor profited, but if he had anything to do with it, he'd acted out of desperation of his plan being found out. At least Mr. York had taken the truth with him to the grave, and that became a win for Mayor Shelton. Minnie now had one neighbor who didn't seem to mind her stupid cows, so she'd hit the jackpot. I didn't believe those were the only three suspects, just the ones I was aware of. The police must have a longer list and I had faith they'd make an arrest soon.

An hour later, I realized I still hadn't seen Belle, so I searched the house. Under beds, behind the curtains, the closets... I looked everywhere and my heart sank when I didn't find her. Maybe she had slipped out, and that worried me more than anything. She'd be a perfect snack for the nighttime predators in our area.

I went out front and yelled for her but only heard a coyote howling in the distance and mosquitoes buzzing around me. Panic gripped me as I raced around the house calling for her with Tinker at my heels. When I got to the garage, I scanned the yard once again while tears welled in my eyes.

Where was she?

Meow.

"Belle!"

I followed the sound and realized it came from inside the garage. As I hurried inside, my throat choked with fear. I flung open the door that connected the laundry room to the kitchen, then the one to the garage, and Belle meowed once again, then scampered past me. I hadn't been able to hear her through the two closed doors.

Tommy. It had to be Tommy, and I had some choice words about him locking Belle in the garage, accident or not.

I pulled out my phone and he picked up on the third ring. I heard a baby crying in the background and it only fueled my anger.

"What's up, Tilly?"

"Were you here at the house today?"

"No. Why?"

"Are you sure, Tommy? I don't like you coming in *my* house without my permission."

"Tilly, I wasn't in your house. I drove down to Oak Peak to get some medicine at the pharmacy since Little River didn't have it. I didn't even go near your place."

I hung up the phone as the tears finally fell and my knees began to shake. I never used the garage, preferring to park my truck right outside. The door was always locked, and if Tommy hadn't been in the house, that only meant one thing.

I dialed my phone again.

"Byron," I said, my voice quaking with fear. "Someone was in my house."

14

After my phone call to Byron, I also contacted Debbie. She actually arrived before him with an overnight bag and a shotgun over her shoulder.

"What are you doing?" I asked as she strode inside. I hadn't been expecting her.

"Me and Big Bertha are staying the night. I've got to get up before the crack of dawn to make tomorrow's donuts, but we'll be here until then. No one messes with my Tilly."

She gave me a hug, and her dedication brought more tears to my eyes.

"You don't worry about anything," Debbie called as she trotted up the stairs to the bedrooms. "We'll take care of you."

Moments later, Byron pulled up, obviously not in any hurry.

"Hey, Tilly," he said, his voice tired. "What's going on?"

"Someone came into my home and locked Belle in the garage," I said. "You sure took your sweet time getting here. Even Debbie beat you, and you know how slow she drives."

He rolled his eyes and sat down at the kitchen table. "Sorry. It's been a long day. A whole herd of cows got loose on the freeway between here and Cedarville. It took hours to round them up. Besides, you didn't call 9-1-1. You called my personal phone, so I assumed you weren't in any danger."

He'd given me his number in an informal way, not for emergencies.

Debbie came down the stairs with Big Bertha still over her shoulder.

"Holy heck, Debbie," Byron said, his eyes widening at the sight of the gun. "Do you have a permit for that?"

"Of course I do. I'm a law-abiding citizen and I'm a very good shot. I'll knock the knickers off anyone who doesn't belong in this house."

She joined us at the table and Byron shook his

head, then pulled out his little notebook. "Tell me what happened, Tilly."

When I finished my story, Debbie pursed her lips together in anger. Byron simply stared at me.

"Was anything taken?"

"Not that I've been able to find."

"Well, are you sure you just didn't leave the front door open? Maybe a breeze came through and locked the cat in the garage?"

"The wind would have had to blow open the door from the kitchen to the laundry room, then the one from the laundry room to the garage."

Debbie snorted and rolled her eyes. "Sounds like a hurricane or tornado would be necessary for that to happen."

"And I never go into the garage," I stated. "I park out front."

Byron sighed and rubbed his hand over his face. "If the perp didn't take anything, then why would someone break in?"

"You're the police, Byron," Debbie said. "That's your job to figure it out."

"It's getting late," he said, standing. "I'll make a report so it's on file. Other than that, there's nothing I can do. You say someone was in your house, but nothing was stolen. It doesn't make any sense, Tilly."

Grinding my jaw in irritation, I got to my feet and headed for the front door. Byron obviously thought I had lost my marbles, but he also had a point. Why break in and not take anything?

"Have a good one," he said, then walked out and got in his cruiser.

After shutting the door, I turned to Debbie. "I feel like I'm an egg short of a dozen. Who's busting into my home and not stealing anything?"

"I don't know," Debbie said. "But let's have some tea and discuss it."

She ran upstairs while I filled the kettle and put it on the stove, then returned with a jigsaw puzzle.

"We're doing a puzzle?" I asked, grabbing the teabags out of the cabinet.

"Yes. They help me focus."

I brought the two mugs over to the table and sat down. Debbie emptied the box and the pieces scattered all over the table. We worked to flip them all upright.

As I sipped my tea, I studied the picture on the box. A cat lay sleeping on a bookcase surrounded by hundreds of tomes. It shouldn't be too difficult.

An hour later, we'd made some progress, but not nearly as much as I thought we would.

"They must have been looking for information," Debbie said. "It's the only thing that makes sense."

I sat back and crossed my arms over my chest. "Like what?"

"You've been reporting on the fireworks and the murder. My guess is that you've come across the person responsible for both and you don't even know it."

"So you think someone came in here to see if I had written something about the murder?"

"Possibly," Debbie said with a shrug. "Maybe they were looking for police reports. Maybe notes you've taken about both incidents. They wanted to see what you know. Was your computer here?"

I shook my head. "No. I had taken it to the office."

Debbie nodded as she glanced over the puzzle again. She picked up a piece that belonged to the cat and moved it around, trying to make it fit.

"They should have taken something because then you'd think it was a robber. With everything in its place, information is the only thing they could be after. And who would know the most? The girl who's got her nose into everything. That's who."

I burst out laughing. "That's the pot calling the kettle black."

"The difference is, you get paid for it. I just get the joy of knowing everything about everyone."

We worked on the puzzle for another brief, quiet stretch, then I raised my hands above my head. "I'm done for the night. I need some sleep."

Debbie picked up another puzzle piece and tried to make it fit. "Here's the thing, Tilly. Pretty soon, all the pieces are going to fall into place and we'll know who lit the fireworks, who killed York, and who broke into your house."

She snapped the piece into its rightful slot. "Just like that," she said with a grin.

THE NEXT MORNING, my alarm went off and I rolled out of bed without disturbing Tinker or Belle. My loving cat had disappeared after I let her out of the garage the previous night and I hadn't stirred when she finally came to bed. I hoped she didn't hold much of a grudge, or I'd come home to a hairball on my pillow or something equally nasty.

I checked Debbie's room, and as promised, she had gone before the dawn; however, she'd left her suitcase and Big Bertha, so she'd be back. It was nice to have such a good friend I could call in times of need, and I wanted to do something special for her. But what did you get the woman who owned the town bakery? Certainly not a cake or a bouquet of cookies. I'd have to think on that one.

My anxiety had ebbed and I actually felt rested and ready in the quiet morning to take on my day... or so I thought until my phone rang and I about sprang out of my own skin. My coffee jumped out of the mug I held and all down the front of my nightshirt.

I did a quick dance around the kitchen as I held the scalding cloth away from my skin, then slipped on the coffee that had made it to the tile. Thankfully I didn't land on my tailbone again, but instead my hip and elbow caught the brunt of it. As I lay on the floor and stared up at the ceiling, Tinker came downstairs and licked the tears streaming down my cheeks.

I'd always been a klutz, but lately, it seemed my life had become a perpetual state of disarray and pain.

After a few moments, I staggered to my feet and found my phone on the counter. Harold had called.

"What's going on?" I said once he answered as I slowly bent my elbow and straightened it, grimacing at the pain. Why was it so hard for me to stay on my feet?

"The sheriff called. You've got an appointment the day after tomorrow at two. He's ready to go on the record."

My earlier enthusiasm had fled the building, but I tried to sound optimistic and excited. "Great, Harold. I'll be there."

"Is everything okay, Tilly?"

"I'm fine. Just took a little spill, but I'll be okay."

"You sure can be clumsy."

I reached down and touched my hip, hissing at the bruise that was already forming. "Yes, I know, Harold. Thanks for that reminder."

After I hung up, I pulled out my laptop and called a few insurance agencies about getting a policy in my own name on the house. Almost all offered the same coverage, so I went with the cheapest and was told I'd get something in the mail within a few days. I tossed the phone onto the counter and limped over to get Tinker and Belle's food bowls. Belle glared at me from under hooded lids from the bottom stair but didn't come any closer.

"I wasn't the one who locked you in there," I said as I filled her bowl. "I get that you're upset. I would be, too. But you're casting your devil eyes at the wrong human."

With their food in place, I hobbled over to the sink to wash my hands. I glanced out the window to find Derek crossing my yard. Before I could duck, he waved to me.

"Darn it," I whispered. Swiping a hand over my hair, I glanced down at my coffee-stained shirt. As the knock sounded at my door, I sighed. I shouldn't care what a potential murderer may think of me, but there wasn't any hiding from him. I had to act as normal as possible in case he really did kill his father. He couldn't know I was on to him.

"Hey, Derek," I said as I opened the door, hoping I sounded friendly enough. "What can I do for you?"

"Can I come in for a second? I found something in my dad's things and wanted your input."

How convenient.

"I'm just ready to get in the shower and get to work," I replied, hoping he'd get the message.

"It'll just take a few minutes. I promise."

His eyes reminded me of emeralds on this summer morning and his smile seemed brighter than the sun. He didn't scare me, but until the murder was solved, he certainly should.

"Okay, just for a minute though," I said, stepping outside. "What's up?"

"Did you know you have something on the front of your shirt?" he asked.

"I do," I replied with a smile. "Thank you for the reminder."

He nodded and held out a piece of paper to me. "I was going through my dad's computer. There's not a lot there. It looks like he used it for email and getting the news, but that's about it. I printed this off his email. Do you know this person? It's from a couple of weeks ago."

"Betty Frank," I murmured as I scanned the address, heading, and date. "She owns Filly Feed."

"Read it," Derek urged.

Dear Henry,

I can't tell you how sad the end of our relationship has made me. I thought you and I would move into our twilight years together. I feel you've taken away my dreams of the future and I'm left to wonder what's wrong with me, why I'm not good enough for you, what she has that I don't. I'm tired of thinking this is my fault, but I'm not going to waste another moment on you.

Remember this, Henry: I don't know who said it, but

hell hath no fury like a woman scorned. You'll get what's coming to you.

"OH, MY GOODNESS," I whispered, bringing my hand to my mouth. I never imagined Betty having such a flair for the dramatic.

"What do you think it means, Tilly? Is it possible she killed my dad?"

My mind spun as I put together the pieces. Betty knew about the fireworks because she was on the committee. She could have lit them to get Mr. York in trouble. Maybe he even saw her do it. She came back and he confronted her, then she stabbed him to hide the truth.

It all fit and I could relate to the tone of the email. I'd cried yesterday over my cheating ex-husband, but I'd never threatened him. I'd thought about it, but never voiced it like Betty had.

"I don't know," I replied as I handed him back the page. "Do you have any idea who he left her for?"

"No. but I can keep looking through his things and see if I can figure it out."

"That sounds good. I have a meeting with the

police tomorrow, so if you want, I can tell them about it."

"If you could, that would be great," Derek said. "I can run another copy of this, so take the email with you and tell them to call me if they need anything else."

"I'm going to be late," I said, opening the door behind me. "I'll call you later in the week and let you know what they said."

"Thanks a lot, Tilly. I appreciate your help."

I stepped inside and locked the door behind me, then reread the email a few times.

Had Derek just discovered the killer, or had he tried to divert my focus from him to a woman distraught over a breakup?

15

ON MY WAY back from delivering the mail that didn't belong to the paper, I debated whether I should stop at the post office and make a complaint. Every day we had bills and letters that were supposed to be taken elsewhere, but I didn't want to get the new sorter in any trouble. And, I did enjoy the walks, especially in the morning when the summer sun wasn't so hot. If I ever lost my job at the paper, maybe I'd look into being a mail carrier. With so much exercise, I'd drop weight for sure.

But the reality was, things were getting ridiculous with all this mail confusion, and I wondered if the new sorter had a disability that made her job difficult, or if she just didn't care. Many business owners were spending their time returning their mis-delivered mail to the rightful owners. When I'd first begun taking mail to the proper addressees, people would laugh. Now, I saw some anger and frustration. Hopefully, Philip would be recovered from his appendectomy soon and get back to work.

As I rounded the corner on to Oak Avenue, I spotted Derek up ahead, right in front of the sandwich shop. Just as I was debating crossing the street to avoid him, a woman I didn't know ran up behind him and planted herself right in his path, then shoved him in the chest.

Interesting.

I picked up my pace. When I was close enough to hear, I turned to the store window and pretended to be engrossed in the selection of hammers and screwdrivers on display, but I could see the pair in the window's reflection.

"That money was supposed to go to me!" the woman yelled. "He promised me!"

"Who are you?" Derek asked, his face contorted in confusion.

"My name's Rachel. Your father was supposed to leave that money to me!"

"I-I have no idea what you're talking about," Derek said. "His lawyer called me and I drove up here for the reading of the will. I didn't even know I was in it."

"Where is it?" she hissed, pushing his chest again. "Where's the *real* will?"

Derek looked around as if he searched for help. I could see Rachel was probably in her sixties. Thin as a rail with shoulder length black and gray hair, I guessed she was who Mr. York had left Betty Frank for. But it seemed odd that he would promise her money when they'd only been dating a few weeks.

Unless he'd been two-timing Betty for a lot longer than she knew.

"The lawyer called *me*," Derek said. "I don't know anything about a real will, just the one that was read to me."

"I watched him sign it!" Rachel shrieked. "He signed the will that left everything to me!"

A crowd had now gathered, but everyone kept their distance. Derek looked desperate for assistance.

"Maybe you should be talking to his lawyer," Derek said, his voice calm. "I don't have anything to do with it."

Rachel burst into tears and placed her head in her hands. "That money was going to help me save my farm. Now... now I don't know what to do. I'm going to lose it all."

Derek, bless him, took the woman into a hug and allowed her to cry all over the front of his shirt. Our gazes met and he shrugged his shoulders. He'd been as surprised by the confrontation as I was.

"Who's his lawyer?" Rachel demanded after a few moments as she stepped away from Derek. "I want to talk to him. Now."

He pulled out his phone and read off a number to her. After she put it in her own phone, she stomped away without another word.

People went back to minding their own business and Derek walked over to me.

"I guess that was who my dad was seeing," he said, stuffing his hands in his front jeans pockets.

"I guess so."

He stared at the sidewalk for a moment before speaking. "I honestly don't know what she's talking about."

"I could see that."

"But why would my dad have one will that she obviously saw him sign, but then have another one, which left everything to me?"

"I have no idea, Derek."

"She was sure upset."

"Yes."

But she could also offer me a new dimension to Mr. York's life and possibly give me insight into his murder.

"I'm going to go talk to her," I said, moving past him to catch up to her.

"Rachel!" I yelled as I jogged down the sidewalk. "Rachel!"

She turned and stopped. As I got closer, I noticed tears still tracked down her cheeks.

"May I talk to you for a minute?" I asked.

"Who are you?"

"My name's Tilly Donner. I work for the Tri-Town Times."

She wiped her nose with her palm and nodded. "I've been reading your articles."

"Thank you. That means a lot to me. Would you mind if we talked about Mr. York?"

"I suppose not," she said.

The woman had the saddest blue eyes I'd ever seen.

"Can I buy you a cup of coffee over at Debbie's Deliciousness?"

"Yes. Thank you."

We crossed the street and walked back toward Debbie's. I didn't see Derek anywhere, and I hoped he hadn't decided he needed a donut after the awkward confrontation. Meeting him at the bakery would only make things weirder.

Debbie arched an eyebrow at me as we entered and began to come around the counter. I shook my head, hoping she'd remain in place.

"Let's sit over there where it's quiet," I said, pointing to the table where I'd interviewed the mayor. "I'll get us some coffee."

While Rachel walked over to the table, I weaved in between the chairs towards the counter.

"Two coffees," I whispered. "And don't ask me any questions right now."

"Is that the woman who was just yelling at Derek York?" Debbie hissed.

I rolled my eyes as I pulled money out of my pocket. Leave it to Debbie to ignore my request. "Yes."

"Let me know what she says."

Like I'd have a choice.

After returning to the table, I sat down, slid the cup over to Rachel, and smiled.

"What do you want to talk about?" she asked, getting right down to the brass tacks.

"You and Mr. York were close," I said. "I couldn't help but overhear you yelling at his son."

She shook her head and took a sip of coffee. "I'd been dating Henry for two years. He had a mini-stroke about a year and a half ago and decided he needed to put his affairs in order, which meant getting a will written up. I was there when he signed it, leaving everything to me."

I tried to settle my features into neutral because I really wanted to drop my jaw to the table. Mr. York had been quite the cheating ladies' man, and I didn't have the heart to tell her he'd been seeing at least one woman behind her back.

How many others could there be?

"Are you okay?" Rachel asked. "You look like you're about to be sick or something."

"I'm fine."

"Henry told me about that no-good kid of his. Always stealing from his parents to feed his drug habit. Never coming to visit. Henry even blamed him for the death of his wife. Said she couldn't take the stress."

I sipped my coffee and waited for her to continue. She had obviously given a lot of thought to Derek and his relationship with his father.

But did she think he killed Mr. York?

"Mark my words, once a druggie, always a drug-gie. I wouldn't be one bit surprised if he had a new will made up, then either forged the signature or forced his dad to sign it, then killed him."

"That's quite the accusation," I murmured. "How can you be sure?"

"I can't!" Rachel said, throwing her hands up. "I can only speculate!"

I nodded and decided to change the direction of the conversation. "So, you and Mr. York were close when he died?"

"Yes. We'd gotten into a fight a couple weeks before and we weren't speaking, but that's happened in the past. We just needed some space. We always came back to each other."

I tried to fit the timeline between Rachel and Betty together, but I couldn't. The only thing that made sense was that Mr. York had been seeing them both at the same time.

"When Henry signed that will, he told me he wanted everything to go to me when he died. He wanted me to be able to keep my farm. I've had some tough times the past two years, but the past six months have been the worst."

"Did he give you money to help you?"

"He did. A little here, a little there."

"That was kind of him."

"Yes. He was a good man."

We finished our coffee in silence. When Rachel abruptly stood, it surprised me.

"I need to get back to Cedarville," she said. "I've got a farm to run."

I nodded and got to my feet. "Thanks so much for talking to me. I hope you get everything worked out."

She waved and walked out of the bakery. Before the door had even closed, Debbie had sat down in her chair.

"Tell me everything."

As I repeated the conversation, Debbie hung on every word.

"Do you think this solidifies that Derek did it?" I asked. "I can't imagine him being evil enough to make a fake will."

"Yeah, that's really cold." Debbie shook her head. "But I do I think it means that we have another person on our list of suspects."

"Who? Rachel?"

"Absolutely."

"Why do you say that?"

"Because Rachel claims *she* was on the will. Her farm hasn't been doing well and she needs the money. If the will was in her name, all she had to do is get York out of the way and she'd become a very rich woman."

I groaned and put my head in my palms. "I didn't think about that. You have an evil mind, Debbie."

"Just trying to help out and make sure all our bases are covered."

"What about the fireworks?" I asked with a sigh. "Mr. York said the person who lit them and the person who stabbed him were one and the same."

"Maybe he was wrong," Debbie said with a shrug. "Maybe he wasn't being truthful. Maybe his mind became confused while he lay dying."

I finished my coffee with Debbie staring at me. Frankly, I was dead tired of thinking about who killed Mr. York, of being scared and looking for a motive for murder in everyone I met who was even remotely connected to the man.

"See, that's the thing about you, Tilly. You've got a good heart and want to believe everyone else does as well. I, on the other hand, have a tendency to look for the worst."

"Why is that?"

"It's just my nature."

"I'll tell the Sheriff our suspicions when I meet with him tomorrow."

"With all we've put together, we've got a really good list of suspects for him. Heck, we've practically done the job for him. Now he just needs to see where the evidence leads."

"He's got to pin this on someone soon," I replied. "It's not like we live in a big city. Sure, we've got a few unsavory characters, but overall, people are honest and hard-working."

"I agree, Tilly. And that's what makes Henry York's death even scarier. We don't know if someone else could be murdered next, or why."

16

I DRESSED in my best slacks and blouse for my interview with the sheriff at the City Hall. Discussing murder was serious business, and I wanted to look nice and professional. I didn't have any of the nervous willies I'd had before my interview at the mayor's office. In fact, I felt pretty confident, and I liked this new me that was emerging. With each passing day, I seemed to be returning to the person I was before Tommy knocked up the waitress. My old self had gone into hiding after that blow.

While waiting in the lobby, I thought about my theories on who had killed Mr. York, hoping Byron had gone over them with his boss so I didn't have to reiterate them once again—but I would if asked.

The email from Betty Frank to Mr. York burned

in my purse. I couldn't wait to show it to the police and see what their reaction would be. Then of course I had to tell them about Rachel from Cedarville and Mr. York's infidelities. I felt bad talking ill of the dead, but he could have been killed in a crime of passion, or because of a need for money. Both were perfect motives for murder.

I hoped the sheriff appreciated all my work. If I were in their shoes, I certainly would. Heck, I now had five perfectly good suspects for them to investigate, handed to them on a silver platter.

"Sheriff Connor will see you now, Matilda," the secretary said with a warm smile.

"You can call me Tilly," I replied, getting to my feet. "Everyone does."

She motioned to a closed door. "Head through there and he'll meet you in the hallway."

I went to pull open the door, but it didn't budge.

"Wait until you hear the click."

When it sounded, I quickly twisted the knob and stepped inside, thankful it didn't bang me in the nose.

I could see an office at the end of the gray hallway that branched out into a T, but the desk was empty and no one came out to greet me. As I walked down the corridor, I noted two open doors on each side of me, but the lights were off so I couldn't see inside. A moment later, Byron rounded the corner at the end of the hall with Sheriff Connor.

"You must be Matilda," he said, his hand outstretched.

"Please call me Tilly," I said as our palms met. Byron stood behind him and eyed me warily, which I found odd. Usually he gazed at me with huge puppy-dog eyes full of infatuation. Maybe he'd gotten over me and moved on to someone else, which was fine by me. I didn't want to date a man who thought chickens were the way to my heart. They may be just fine for some women, but not me.

"Let's go in here," the sheriff said, pointing to the open door to my left.

When he flipped on the light, I realized he had led me to an interrogation room. Three metal chairs sat around a large matching table. Why in the world didn't he take me to the office?

"Have a seat, Tilly," Byron said after closing the door behind us.

The sheriff took the chair across from me while Byron remained by the door. An unsettling feeling came over me, but I grinned and pulled my notebook from my bag, determined to write a good article for the paper.

"Thanks for meeting me, Sheriff Connor," I said. "I was hoping I could get some updates on Mr. York's murder... just let the folks of the Tri-Towns know where you are with it."

He nodded and stroked his gray beard. "Byron here tells me that you've been quite the source for information."

A blush crawled from my neck to my cheeks. "Yes, well, I feel I have a civic duty and a social obligation to turn over any information that falls into my lap."

"That's very wise of you, Tilly. Now, it's my understanding that you've come up with three different suspects."

"Well, actually, I'm up to five. Mr. York's son inherited a lot of money, so he definitely needs to be investigated. My neighbor Minnie fought with Mr. York about her cows being in his yard, and she was also part of the secret committee the mayor had put together, so she knew about the fireworks. What better way to get back at him than to light them? He'd be in a boatload of trouble for it. I also heard her tell my other neighbor, Mr. Rupert, that she'd bury a knife in him if he ever hurt her cows."

"Really?"

"Yes. Heard it with my own ears."

"How interesting. Please, go on, Tilly."

"Sure. Then of course, you have the mayor himself. He was getting some pushback from the committee on bringing back the Fourth of July party and he was the one who'd asked Mr. York to hold the fireworks. With his own committee turning on him, he could have wanted to get rid of the fireworks and accidentally killed Mr. York."

"Who else did you have in mind?"

With him and Byron not taking any notes, how in the world were they going to remember all I had to say?

Maybe Byron had written down what I'd told him already.

"Well, Mr. York had two girlfriends. The first was Betty Frank." I reached into my bag and pulled out the email. "Derek York gave this to me two days ago. If that's not a direct threat, I don't know what is."

The sheriff slid the paper to his side of the table and glanced over it. "Betty Frank down at Filly Feed?"

"Yes. She was also on the committee and had a big fight with the mayor. With Mr. York dumping her, she definitely had motive to get back at him and says right in that email that she's going to."

He slid the email printout back over to me.

"You can keep that if you want," I said. "Derek gave me the copy and I told him I'd be passing it on to you. It could be important evidence."

Sheriff Connor narrowed his gaze on me. "How very kind of you. And you said there was one other person?"

"A woman from Cedarville named Rachel. I didn't get her last name. She had a big fight with Derek York right on Oak Avenue yesterday. She says that Mr. York was supposed to leave all his money to her. She's also having financial troubles. She could have killed him, thinking she'd be the beneficiary, and come into a bunch of money."

"Wow. Quite a selection of perpetrators there," he replied.

"Like I said, I feel it's my civic duty to pass along what I hear. So, why don't we get to the interview?"

"Yes, let's do that. Tell me about the morning you found York."

I glanced up at Byron. "He's already taken my statement."

"I'd like to hear it from you, Tilly, if you don't mind."

As I cleared my throat, I became uncomfortable and wiggled in my seat. Something wasn't right. "Well, I was on my way to work and decided to stop by to see how his chat with Byron went the previous night."

I told the sheriff as much as I could remember and didn't leave out any details.

"And how did you come up with all these other suspects?" he asked.

I looked at Byron again. He leaned against the wall with his arms crossed over his chest, his stare on me.

"Well, I found out information from different people and just kind of put it all together—like a puzzle, I guess."

"And who are your sources for all this information you gathered?"

Suddenly, the room became very warm. "I... I thought *I* was interviewing *you* on the murder. Not the other way around."

"We'll get to that," the sheriff said with a smile. "You've just provided Byron with so much potential evidence, I had to hear it for myself. And here you are bringing me even more suspects. You're really in tune with the pulse of the community for all these people to be giving you so much information."

The longer I sat under his condescending stare, the more uncomfortable I became and the stupider I felt. For a while, I had thought myself so darn smart spinning all the possible suspects and their motives, then passing them on to Byron as if I were doing the police department a favor. Now I wasn't so sure. Maybe I'd just been plain foolish playing detective.

Sheriff Connor sat back and crossed his arms over his chest. "All these theories you've given us... who's your source?"

My cheeks burned as I stared at the tabletop. Did I really want to admit that my friend, Debbie, had provided me with a bunch of gossip? That I'd over-heard conversations? That my mind kept me up at night as I tossed ideas around?

Maybe we'd let our imaginations get the best of us. Had the horror and excitement of a murder propelled me into looking for clues that weren't there?

"I can't give out my sources, Sheriff," I replied, straightening my shoulders. He wouldn't see me wilt under the pressure of ridicule. "However, I would like to get back to the reason for my visit: I'm supposed to be interviewing you for the paper."

"Well, go right ahead," he said. "Ask me your questions."

"Have you gathered a lot of evidence in this case?"

I twisted the pen between my fingers, itching to take some notes and get the interview back on track.

"No comment."

Okay, then.

"Do you have a motive for the murder?"

"No comment."

I glanced up at him and found him smiling at me like I was the dumbest little girl he'd come across in a long time.

I pursed my lips together as I poised my pen over the paper once again. "I'm not asking you to name anyone, but do you have any suspects?"

He shook his head. "No. We're waiting for the local gossip vine to solve the case for us. Nothing is more scientific and accurate than a bunch of hens clucking about their theories and passing those on to the police, who have actually been *trained* in solving murders."

Byron burst out laughing and covered his mouth as if he tried to hide it. A mighty poor job of it.

"You aren't going to tell me anything, are you?" I asked over their chuckling.

"I think we're done here," the sheriff said as he stood. "I had to hear your nonsense for myself, but let me tell you something, Matilda."

My anger flamed as I gripped my pen in my

palm. I wanted to stab the rude, condescending, sexist jerk with it.

"When someone starts pointing the finger at everyone else, it makes me wonder what they have to hide."

"What in the world does that mean?"

He leaned over the table, planting his palms in the middle of it with so much force, the table rattled.

"It means, be careful where you cast your stones, little lady," he growled. Gone were the pleasantries, and I realized he'd been playing with me all along. He had no intention of giving an interview for the paper. He'd brought me into the office to ridicule me.

I narrowed my gaze at him, unable to believe what I was hearing. "Are you saying you think I killed Mr. York?"

"It's a distinct possibility, Ms. Donner. You sure have a lot of theories you're feeding us. Maybe it's to cover up your own guilt? After all, you were the one who found him, right?"

I slowly stood and shoved my notebook in my bag, my cheeks feeling like they'd caught fire. "I didn't kill Mr. York, Sheriff. That's the stupidest thing I've heard all day."

Probably not the best idea to tell the sheriff he

was stupid, but it had slipped out.

He arched an eyebrow at me. "I don't see how it's any dumber than your theories, Ms. Donner."

I didn't bother to ask if he had finished with me. Instead, I walked to the door and stared down Byron, who didn't move.

"Excuse me," I said through clenched teeth. "Unless you're arresting me, I'd like to leave now."

He glanced over my shoulder at his boss, then stepped aside.

I yanked on the door with a sweaty hand.

"Make sure you don't leave town!" the sheriff called to me as I marched toward the lobby.

My body shook with anger. How dare he tell me I'm dumb? How dare he insinuate I had anything to do with Mr. York's murder?

I said nothing as I walked, but wondered if I was truly on the sheriff's shortlist of people, or if he'd been teasing me in hopes I'd back off?

Was it possible that I was getting close to figuring out the killer, and maybe the man was protecting him or her?

Maybe he wasn't the good guy and the conspiracy ran deeper than I could ever imagine.

It would make sense the mayor would have law enforcement on his side.

17

I RETURNED to work from the sheriff's office with shaking hands and the desire to hit something.

"Why is your face so red?" Harold asked as I set down my bag on my desk. "You look like you may blow your top."

"The interview didn't go well," I grumbled.

"Why is that?"

"Because, the sheriff is a pig."

"What happened?" Harold asked with a chuckle.

Usually, I tried not to speak ill of people, but Connor had really gotten under my skin. I sat down behind my desk and told Harold everything. He tapped his pen on a pad of paper and listened intently until I finished.

"Well, that was quite rude of him," he said.

"I was only trying to help. That's all I ever wanted to do. Mr. York's death and the fire upset me more than I can tell you. I want both cases solved."

"We all do, Tilly. No one likes thinking a murderer could be living among us, that he or she may be standing behind us in the line at the grocery store."

"So why was he being such a jerk?"

Harold sighed. "I don't know. He probably feels a little upstaged by you right now. You've got all these theories and suspects while he's sitting around twiddling his thumbs trying to pin this on someone while dealing with his other duties."

"I think finding a killer is more important than wayward cows and kids drinking in the forest on Friday night."

"You're preaching to the choir, my friend. However, he is the sheriff and you're a reporter who isn't supposed to be solving the case—just reporting on it."

I sighed and picked up the stack of mail. The first letter on top was for the barber shop.

"Why don't you stay under the radar for a while, Tilly? Try to forget about the murder and let the sheriff do his job."

Harold rose from his chair and walked over to

my desk. "The cheerleaders over at the high school are having a rose bush sale and asked if we could write a piece on it for the paper. You can call Mrs. Woodsley, the head of the cheer department, and find out the particulars. Get a couple of quotes while you're at it—what they're going to do with the money, etcetera."

I took the slip of paper and dialed the number, thankful for something to keep my mind off the sheriff.

Two hours later, I had my article written and my faith in humanity had been restored. The cheerleaders had teamed up with the track team and decided to do something useful this summer while waiting for school to start. They intended to use the money they raised as a donation to the food bank over in Cedarville that served the Tri-Town area.

As I looked over the final draft before handing it off to Harold, the front door flew open and Betty Frank entered.

With wide, furious eyes and hands fisted at her sides, she glanced around until our gazes locked.

"You!" she shrieked as she marched over to my

desk. I shot to my feet and scrambled behind my chair.

"What's going on?" Harold asked, hurrying over.

Betty turned to him. With anger radiating off her and her hawkish nose, she looked like she wanted to peck his eyes out.

"This has nothing to do with you," she yelled. "I'm here to see her!"

Both of them stared at me.

"W-what's going on?" I stuttered.

Betty planted both palms on my desk and leaned forward. "Guess who just came to visit me?"

"I have no idea."

"Sheriff Connor!"

Uh-oh.

"How dare you give my name to the police? You come into my store and ask me questions that aren't any of your business and then you do this?"

Harold arched an eyebrow at me, stepping back. I'd gotten myself into this mess, and he had no intention of helping me out.

"I'm a law-abiding citizen," Betty said, shaking her finger at me as spittle flew from her mouth onto my desk. "There isn't any reason for you to suspect me of murdering Henry York. What did I do to you to deserve this? People are going to start talking and they'll think I did it! Do you understand what that will do to my reputation?"

Guilt washed through me as Betty railed on. I never expected Sheriff Connor to tell any of the suspects I'd mentioned where he got the information. He obviously had every intention of making me look even more foolish and turning the townspeople against me.

"Why in the world would you tell the sheriff that I had something to do with the murder?"

After a brief stretch of silence, I realized she expected me to answer.

I cleared my throat and glanced over her shoulder at Harold. He stared at me expectantly, waiting for me to speak.

"Well, Mr. York's son, Derek, gave me an email he found on his daddy's computer."

I hoped she'd understand and I wouldn't have to continue. Did she really want Harold to know that Mr. York had cheated on her?

"And? I sent Henry a lot of emails. What does this have to do with anything?"

"In this... particular email, you threatened him." I reached down into my bag and retrieved the piece of paper, then opened it. "It says, '*Remember this, Henry: I don't know who said it, but hell hath no fury like a woman scorned. You'll get what's coming to you.'"*

Both Harold and I stared at Betty. Her skin paled as her breath hitched. The anger seemed to be seeping from her bones like water through a sieve.

"I... I didn't mean I wanted him dead," she whispered. "We had a relationship. He left me for another woman. I was just... talking. I meant that karma would come for him, not that I was going to stab him."

"Derek asked me to give this to the police," I said. "It's not an accusation I just pulled out of thin air."

"Oh, Lord," she whispered. "What am I going to do?"

"I'm sure everything is going to be fine," I said, coming around my desk. "The sheriff is just doing what he should—following up on a lead. If you're innocent, you'll be in the clear."

"No one is going to want to buy feed for their animals from a murder suspect."

I glanced over at Harold and he stepped up behind Betty. "I'm sure no one even knows what the sheriff was talking to you about. Everything will be fine."

"We all know that's not true," she said.

"It's going to be fine," he repeated.

"You shouldn't have turned that letter in," Betty said, her glare once again glacial. "Henry's boy could have come to me and asked me about it. You could have done the same. Now my reputation is ruined."

"But no one knows the cops were even talking to you about the murder," I said, trying to sound reasonable.

"You know how this town is. The walls have ears. Everyone will know by this time tomorrow."

She stormed out, leaving Harold and me staring at each other.

"You shouldn't have done that, Tilly," Harold said. "You should have asked her about it."

We both returned to our desks. As I rubbed my temples, I tried to convince myself I'd done the right thing.

"What if she is the murderer?" I asked. "What if she's just playing the innocent card?"

"If that's the case, she's pretty good at it."

"The sheriff made me feel like I'm an absolute idiot, but here he is investigating the list of suspects I gave him."

"There's that as well," Harold said. "I believe he'd be negligent if he didn't. You've got a good head on your shoulders and you're smart. You had evidence fall into your lap and you did the right thing. But, I still think you should have talked to Betty."

As I considered the rest of my suspects, a sinking feeling settled in the pit of my stomach. If Connor told all of them that I'd been the one to give him their names, I had four more people who were going to hate me.

"I'm going to deliver the wayward mail," I mumbled.

The walk would hopefully clear my head.

I couldn't shake the guilt about Betty being so upset. Maybe I'd gotten a little ahead of myself. Maybe my imagination had run wild and gotten the best of me. The self-doubt ate at me even more than the guilt. Had I gone off the deep end looking for suspects and motives? Had I stuck my nose where it didn't belong?

Despite my pleasant hello and a smile, the owner of the barber shop glared at me when I handed him his mail. Considering he used to be very friendly, I guessed he'd heard that I gave Betty Frank's name to the police. The gossip vine had caught fire once again, but this time, it was against me.

I'd been its victim once before when Tommy left. Except that time, I saw pity in people's gazes. Even while passing people on the street on my way back to the office, I noted the sideways glances or the outright scowls of anger.

"You've really stepped in it this time," I mumbled as I opened the office door.

But deep in my gut, I knew I'd been right to turn over the names of the potential killers. Each had a good reason to murder Mr. York. Each knew about the fireworks.

People may be mad at me now and consider me the town snitch. However, when the sheriff solved the case and put someone in cuffs, they'd change their tune.

I just hoped one of the names I'd given the police was that of the killer.

18

"THAT'S JUST RUDE," Debbie said from my kitchen table. "I can't believe that jerk sheriff called us clucking hens. You'd think we were in our seventies sitting on our porches with nothing better to do than gossip. I run a successful business. You write for the darn paper. We are *not* old hens."

"I know," I replied as I set out some bacon-wrapped peppers. Carla was coming over and we were going to play some cards. The three of us hadn't been together much since Carla got back from her cruise, and I looked forward to the evening. "I couldn't believe it either. He's sure nice around re-election time, though. I remember he stopped by the paper a few days before voting day and was kissing

Harold's behind looking for an endorsement. He was very kind to me then. Nothing like yesterday."

"Are you going to write about how he treated you?"

"No, I don't think so. If I did, it would come across as me attacking him. Maybe even desperate or that I can't handle a little insult from him. Besides, Betty Frank made sure everyone knew I gave her name to the police. I'm not exactly popular right now. If I wrote something derogatory about the sheriff, everyone would think we were in some big fight, and I'm not about to go there."

A knock sounded at the door and Tinker raced in to see who it was. I opened it and gave Carla a big hug. "Hey," I said. "I'm glad you could make it tonight."

"Me too. I brought us some burritos to munch on while we play."

Carla managed the Mexican restaurant in Cedarville. Not only was it the only Mexican restaurant in the Tri-Town area, but the food couldn't be beat. We'd had a competitor move into Little River last year, and he hadn't lasted six months. My mouth salivated at the smells wafting from the tin.

"Oh, I love those things," Debbie said. Standing,

she gave Carla a squeeze. "Thanks for bringing them."

Once we were settled around the table with full plates, Carla asked, "So what's new on Mr. York's murder?"

I hadn't had a chance to tell her about Betty Frank's email or my confrontation with her. When I laid it out for her, she stared at me, stunned.

"Oh, my word," Carla murmured. "She always seemed so nice."

"I'd never been in her store until Byron gave me the chickens," I said. "I knew who she was, but I'd never met her. She definitely didn't seem like a murderer, or a woman scorned."

"To be truthful, none of the people on our list do," Debbie replied. "They all seem like nice, decent folks. Minnie may be a little off her rocker with her love for those cows, but I don't think she'd hurt anyone over them."

"I don't know about that," I said. "If she got angry enough, I think she might. Those cows are like her babies now that her son is away in college. She obviously needed something to dote over, and for some reason, she's chosen the cows. And, she threatened to stab Bill Rupert if he caused them any harm."

"That's really weird," Carla said. "Really, really weird."

"The mayor has a mean streak," I said. "And the most to lose, namely re-election and being top dog in this town. Trying to cover up the fireworks was the smartest thing he could have done. It could have just gone wrong and he accidentally lit them."

"That's true," Carla said. "But how do you accidentally light a firework? It's not like it's a cow patty you slip on or a door that knocks you in the face."

I rolled my eyes as she and Debbie laughed. I'd never told them about the coffee accident, so they didn't know the bruise on my hip had turned a horrible black/purple color. Thankfully, the lump on my head had faded to yellow and could be hidden with a little makeup.

"You're a funny one, Carla," I replied. "Good thing I like you or I'd drag you over to Minnie's and shove your face right in one of those patties."

Debbie let out a long whistle. "Maybe you are the murderer, Tilly. That's a pretty serious threat!"

We all giggled, and it felt so good to be with my friends once again.

"Derek York just became very wealthy," Carla said. "He's the guilty one in my eyes."

"But Mr. York said the person who lit the fireworks and the person who stabbed him were one and the same," I replied, cutting up my burrito. "He would have had to light the fireworks, hide, then come back and stab his father. It doesn't really fit."

"I don't know what to think about that. Maybe York was hallucinating," Debbie said, wiping her mouth with a paper towel. "Derek has the most to gain. A million dollars is a lot of money."

"And as you brought up, then there's that Rachel woman," I said.

"Who's Rachel?" Carla asked.

She listened intently as we filled her in.

"Well, that's an interesting twist," Carla said. "I wonder if they'll be any other women coming around saying Mr. York promised them a stack of cash."

"She says Derek York must have forged a will, then killed his father," I said.

"Or, Rachel thought she was still the beneficiary and she couldn't wait around for Henry to die, so she took care of things herself," Debbie mused.

"What a tangled web," Carla said. "And the police didn't mention anything about getting closer to finding the suspect?"

I told her about my visit to the police station.

"Unbelievable. I'm never voting for that toad again."

"All I know is that I'm tired of being afraid of everything," I said. "I don't know if two of my neighbors are murderers and then someone coming into my home... that really crossed the line."

"Did you ever find anything missing?" Carla asked.

"Not a thing. I don't have anything valuable. Just my stuff, and I have no idea who would want any of it. Heck, sometimes I really study this house and realize I don't want some of the things in here."

"Why is that?" Carla asked. "You have a really nice, comfortable home."

"I guess it's because of Tommy," I said with a sigh. "Sometimes I look around and remember what we were supposed to have: a long life together and some kids. I worked hard to get this house ready for that, and now when I think about my ex and what he did I... I just don't like living here. It reminds me of the past."

"Then change it," Debbie said. "Instead of thinking of it as a family home, make it your own."

I thought of my big paycheck that still needed to

be deposited, which would allow me some new paint. I could also sew some new curtains, recover the couch, paint some of the furniture... maybe I should consider an overhaul, even if the house was way too big for just me. Maybe in the future there'd be someone to share it with.

"We can help you," Carla said. "Maybe you can turn one of the bedrooms upstairs into your office or a craft room. Something *you* want."

Well, those bedrooms were supposed to be filled with kids, but maybe they were right. Maybe it was time to let go of what could have been, what I had coveted then, and move forward to what I wanted now. But frankly, I wasn't sure what that would be.

"And you know Mac will take down a wall or two for you," Carla said. "He loves doing home remodels."

"I'll think about it," I said, eyeing the wall that separated the kitchen from the living room. Maybe it would be nice to have it removed and just have one large living area. "Let's finish eating and then play some cards."

The conversation moved to the gossip Debbie had heard during the day while working. The Physical Education coach at the Oak Peak High School had been caught kissing the math teacher over at Little River High School. Not exactly scandalous except for the fact he'd been dating an insurance agent in Cedarville, who still didn't know about the kiss.

"I'm sure someone will tell her," Debbie said. "Then we'll wait and see what happens."

"What are you expecting?" Carla asked.

"Well, I looked her up on social media. She's got a bunch of memes about cheating husbands and how worthless they are. Stuff about burning down houses and getting revenge. She might go off the deep end and slash his tires."

"Wouldn't that be something," Carla said, shaking her head. "Hopefully that would be the worst of it and she doesn't do anything too horrible."

"Like what?" I asked.

Carla shrugged. "Pull out her gun and shoot him. I don't know."

I ate the last of my burrito trying to recall what I'd done when Tommy had told me he was leaving for another woman. I'd cried a lot and begged him stay. It had never occurred to me to hurt him. I'd been paralyzed by his betrayal.

"Well, maybe they'll be able to settle it peacefully," I said. "If there's even anything to settle. For all we know, they've been broken up."

"Oh, I don't think so," Debbie said. "Her online status still says she's in a relationship. She's pretty active on social media, so I imagine that would change right away if they'd separated."

We discussed the kiss for another half-hour. It relieved me to focus on someone else's problems instead of Mr. York's murder and me being labeled the town snitch. Curiosity and fear had been consuming me. With my friends sitting around my kitchen table eating burritos, drinking iced tea, and talking about other people, my world felt normal once again.

I rose from the table and cleared the plates. After quickly rinsing them, I arranged them in the dish-washer while Debbie and Carla kept chatting away.

"Don't forget I brought donuts for dessert," Debbie said.

"What kind?" Carla asked.

"I've got a new banana filling I'm trying out. I also brought a sugar-free one for you, Tilly."

I turned and smiled. "That was sweet, Debbie. How did you know I'm not eating any sugar?"

Debbie rolled her eyes. "You come see me almost every day, and almost every day you have a donut.

But lately, you've been skipping them." She tapped her finger against her temple. "I'm perceptive, Tilly. I see everything and take mental notes."

Of course she did. That's why she was the go-to for information on the townspeople. "Well, thanks. I appreciate it."

I reached into the refrigerator and pulled out two pink boxes, both with a *Debbie's Deliciousness* label on them, but one also had sugar free written across the top.

"I've been thinking about making a sugar-free line of donuts anyway," she continued. "Just to see what happens. People around here are starting to get fat, so I think that would be good for them and for my pocketbook. I'm working with different sweeteners, so be honest with me on your opinion about it."

"I will."

After placing the box on the counter, I pulled out some plates and decided I'd have half the donut now and save the other half for tomorrow.

I opened the regular donuts and set them on plates for my friends, then brought them over to the table.

When I returned to the counter, I lifted the lid on my box, then opened my knife and spatula drawer, which was horribly disorganized, containing a mish-mash of gadgets. I really needed to straighten it out.

Something in the back caught my eye. My heart thundered as I slowly reached for it, like I would if it were a snake about to strike. I pulled out a knife.

I stared at the red and blue pattern of the hilt for a moment, trying to figure out where I'd seen it before.

It wasn't my knife.

My hands began to tremble when it all finally came to me. It was the same pattern I'd seen on the knife sticking out of Mr. York's chest.

I dropped it and it clanked to the floor.

"What was that?" Carla asked.

Shaking my head, I couldn't answer her.

"Did you drop a knife?" Debbie asked after walking over. "You're darn lucky you didn't stab your foot."

"That doesn't belong to me," I whispered.

Debbie laid her hand on my shoulder. "What do you mean?"

"It's not mine."

"Who does it belong to?" Carla asked as she bent down and picked it up. "I think you better sit down, Tilly. You look like you've just seen the Devil himself."

I nodded and shuffled over to my chair. Debbie and Carla also took their seats. We all stared at the knife Carla had put down between us.

Was I losing my mind?

I placed my head in my hands and closed my eyes for a moment. Recalling finding Mr. York, I was certain that this knife possessed the same decoration as the one that had been in his chest.

"You're scaring me, Tilly," Carla whispered. "What's going on?"

I glanced at my friends, then back at the knife. "That's not mine, but it looks exactly like the one that killed Mr. York."

A heavy silence fell over us while we all stared at the offending object.

"And now it's... it's in your house?" Debbie asked incredulously.

"Y-yes," I replied as I thought over events from the past couple of days. "Whoever locked Belle in the garage must have been the one to hide it in the drawer."

"Someone's trying to frame you," Carla said. "They're trying to pin the murder on you."

"I didn't do it," I said, looking at my friends. "I didn't kill Mr. York, and I didn't light those fireworks."

"Of course you didn't," Debbie said. "To be safe, let me take this home tonight."

My stomach twisted in knots as I tried to think logically. My friends didn't have anything to do with any of this, did they? I wanted to believe they didn't so badly, but my nerves were frayed and I didn't trust anyone—not my neighbors, not my friends.

And I felt really bad about that.

Debbie could take it home and say she found it in my house. But then again, how would she know that it matched the murder weapon?

She wouldn't. I hadn't told her about the knife, but then again, Debbie knew everything. For all I knew, she'd seen photos of the murder scene from someone who worked in the police department.

I needed these women. I needed to trust someone. If my friends weren't involved, I also wanted to protect them. It had become apparent that someone was trying to pin Mr. York's death on me, and I wasn't going to take it.

"I'm going to keep it here," I said.

"Tilly, that's just inviting trouble!" Carla said. "Someone came in here and put that in your drawer!"

"I know. But they obviously have a plan for me.

They don't know that I've found it, and I'm going to beat them at their own game."

Debbie sighed and shook her head. "You don't even know what game you're playing."

"I agree," I said with a sigh. "Hopefully, I can figure out the rules before it's my turn to make a move."

19

TWO DAYS PASSED and nothing happened, but I
wasn't sure what I was waiting for. I hadn't wanted to
go to work and leave my house unattended while I
anticipated the killer's next move, so I'd told Harold I
was having some female issues and I didn't feel well
enough to head into the office. He sent me some
Letters to the Editor to edit. I found some of them
quite interesting and they helped keep my mind off
the knife I'd found in my drawer.

The people who actually bothered to write in
were of two camps in regard to the fireworks: they
either thought bringing back the Fourth of July celebration was a great idea, or they vehemently
opposed it. Almost every letter cited the article I'd
written after interviewing the mayor, which really

made me feel good. People were reading what I wrote, and it resonated with them.

However, I could also see the town becoming heatedly divided on the subject, which was never a good thing. I'd witnessed it once before when they'd put in the stoplight on Oak Avenue last year, right in the middle of town. Personally, I thought it had been needed with the speeders and those who texted while driving. Mrs. Marple, a lifelong resident in her seventies, had almost been mowed down while trying to cross during her shopping day. After the incident, she'd marched right over to Mayor Shelton's office and demanded something be done. Considering her ancestors had been founding members of the town many generations ago, they mayor had been inclined to listen. Since I worked right on Oak Avenue, I witnessed the challenges the pedestrians faced on a regular basis. On some days, heavy prayer became mandatory before crossing.

But there were plenty who held opposing views from me. Mainly, the speeders and those who didn't focus on the road.

People yelled at each other in the diner, friends and family didn't speak to each other, and everyone felt the need to voice their opinion. Some said it would only clog up the street, while others agreed with me that it would potentially save lives. The city council had voted to put in the stoplight to help slow traffic down the main drag, and once it had gone up, the debates began to ebb. After a while, everyone accepted it and went on with their lives.

The fireworks controversy felt the same to me. Both sides seemed ingrained in their stance and no one wanted to listen to each other.

As far as the murder, the townspeople who wrote in pressured the sheriff to do his darn job and solve the crime. Some were scared to death and looked at everyone they came in contact with as a potential killer. They didn't want to leave their homes. Others thought Mr. York had been murdered by a transient who was now long gone. The major consensus was that it had been ten years since the last murder, and the world was going to hell in a handbasket.

My stepdad always said that opinions were like behinds: everyone had one.

I also wanted the murder solved, as long as I wasn't the main suspect.

While I was fixing myself a cup of tea at the kitchen sink on day three of my self-imposed quarantine, I noted two police cruisers coming down the road by Mr. York's. My heart beat a little faster as they passed his house and rolled down my driveway kicking up a bunch of dust.

I hurried to close the windows in the living room, but I was too late. A plume of dirt filtered in through the screens. How disrespectful. They could have come at a much slower pace and I wouldn't have to dust tomorrow.

Belle hissed and ran for the stairs. Tinker barked. The police exited their cars and sauntered up my steps.

"What the holy heck?" I mumbled as I hurried to the front door. They wanted me.

I opened the door to find the sheriff, Byron, and two other deputies I recognized, but I didn't know their names.

"Matilda Elizabeth Donner?" Sheriff Connor asked.

"You know exactly who I am, Sheriff," I replied, crossing my arms over my chest. Could he see my heart thumping through my T-shirt?

"We have a warrant to search your home."

I felt like I'd just entered one of Carla's crime shows, and I wished I could remember what to say.

"Based on what?" I squeaked, my throat closing around the words.

"Based on an anonymous tip we received."

"A tip on what?"

"That someone has seen a replica of the knife used to kill Mr. York in your house."

I narrowed my gaze at him as he grinned, realizing he enjoyed coming into my home uninvited.

"Please take a seat out here on the terrace, Mrs. Donner, and bring the dog with you."

"Fine." Brushing by him, I sat on my porch swing. "Tinker, go outside, girl. Don't let my cat out of the house, Sheriff. And Byron, you better stay out of my underwear drawer."

The sheriff cast me a confused look while Byron blushed a deep red, then hurried into the house.

As Tinker tore around the corner to see her chickens, I stared at the York place and tried not to think about what was going on within my own. They'd never find the supposed weapon. I'd made sure of that.

But who had called in the anonymous tip?

I thought about my run-in with Betty Frank. If it had been her, that meant she had also murdered Mr. York. There was no way it had been a coincidence that the knife planted in my drawer was the same design as the one used to kill Mr. York. But my altercation with her had happened *after* the break-in, so it didn't make sense that she had anything to do with the knife I found. It had to be someone else, but who?

About fifteen minutes passed and Derek came out the front door and walked across his portion of land, slid under the fence, and continued onto mine. He didn't wave or smile, but instead shoved his hands into the front pockets of his jeans as he glanced at the police cruisers.

Now, I'd given a lot of thought to who had planted that knife, and Derek happened to be high on the list. Someone wanted me to go down for the murder of Mr. York. I would be an easy target for Derek. All he had to do was wait until I left, then break in. If he'd stolen from his parents before, he knew how to jimmy a lock.

How darn convenient for him.

"What's going on, Tilly?" he asked from the bottom of the porch.

I didn't bother to try to hide anything or sugar-coat it. "The police showed up with a warrant and are searching my house."

"For what?"

"Apparently, they received a tip that I have a replica of the knife that killed your daddy."

His eyes widened. Today they looked as blue as

the sea. How in the world did that happen? "Really? They think you killed him?"

"I guess so," I replied with a shrug and a sigh.

"Is that legal? For them to barge into your house like that?"

"Sheriff Connor has a warrant, so I assumed it was legal, but I honestly don't know."

"Have you called a lawyer?" he asked as he ascended the stairs.

"Pfft. I don't know any lawyers, and besides, aren't they really expensive?"

"Let me call mine." He pulled his phone from his back pocket. "I think you need representation."

I was about to argue, but maybe he was right. In every television show I'd seen, they called a lawyer when they could, especially if the bad guy got hauled down to the police station.

Derek turned away from me and headed down the steps as he talked. A few minutes passed and he hung up, then came up onto the porch again. "Can I sit?"

"Sure."

He was keeping an eye on things, either because he wanted to make certain I went to prison for the murder, or he truly cared about the injustice that had befallen me.

"What did the lawyer say?" I asked as I plucked a cuticle.

"He doesn't want you to say anything to the police. If they take you in, I'm supposed to call him back and he'll meet us at the station."

"Why are you doing this for me?"

He shrugged and sighed. "It seems like you're the only person in this town who doesn't want money from me. You either like me or hate me for who I am, whether I have money or not. And, I can't tell which one it is—like or hate."

I decided to ignore the last comment, because I didn't know myself. It all depended on whether he killed his daddy and set me up to take the fall. I did want to like him, but I wasn't going to be one of those women who fell in love with a criminal and visited them in prison on Sunday's and called the relationship the greatest love story of the century.

"Who wants your money?" I asked.

"Don't you think the question should be, how did everyone find out my dad left me a bunch of money?"

"Oh, no," I replied. "That's easy to answer. Barb down at the bank. She called my friend Debbie, and after that, your inheritance didn't stand a chance at being kept a secret."

Derek chuckled and shook his head. "Figures. I've got the sewing club, the high school football team, and the book club calling me for donations. It seems like every woman from the age of twenty and up is also eyeing me." He turned to meet my gaze. "Except you."

Little butterflies tickled my stomach and I turned away. I didn't have the heart to tell him I thought he could be the murderer. He'd just hired his lawyer for me.

"Well, good luck with all those women. I'm sure you'll find one you like."

"I think I already have."

Was that a pang of jealousy slapping my chest, or nerves from the situation inside my house?

"Good. I'm happy for you."

We sat in silence for a long time, our feet moving in tandem to keep the swing swaying. If the murder hadn't been hanging over our heads, I would say it could have been a nice afternoon. In fact, I would have offered him some iced tea. But instead, I worried and wondered about what the police would find in my house. After discovering the knife, I searched every square inch looking for something else that could have been planted but found nothing. However, that didn't mean the police wouldn't, and this made me terribly nervous.

"Did you read the warrant?" Derek asked.

"No. The sheriff just said he was there for the supposed knife I'm hiding."

"How much longer do you think they'll be?"

"I don't know, Derek," I replied, rolling my eyes. "I've never had my house searched by the police before."

"Right. Sorry about that."

The sheriff came out a few minutes later, empty-handed. Trailed by his deputies, he stared at me with irritation.

"Did you find what you're looking for?" I asked, getting to my feet.

"We'll be in touch," he grumbled as they all filed down the stairs.

"I'd take that as a no," Derek murmured.

We watched the two police cruisers drive away, and then he turned to me. "I'll head home now. I'm glad everything worked out for you, but if you need my lawyer, call me."

"Thank you," I said, my eyes welling with tears. Was it from his kindness, or from relief the police didn't find anything? I hadn't realized how tense I'd been waiting for the verdict.

I really liked Derek, but I trusted him as much as I trusted my stupid chickens not to peck my legs. Maybe after the murderer was caught, I could get to know him a little better. If he was going to be my neighbor, it would be a good idea to become friendly with him.

With a sigh, I walked around the house to the chicken coop and found Tinker with her nose through the wires once again. This time, the chickens each lay right next to her snout, but didn't peck her. They turned their heads and stared up at me.

"You two are good for something besides the eggs," I mumbled, crossing my arms over my chest.

Little did the sheriff or Deputy Byron know, I'd buried the knife right under the stupid chickens after Debbie and Carla had left that night.

The two hens may very well have just saved me from prison, so I decided to keep them.

20

THE POLICE HAD BEEN gentle with my things, not like in the television shows where they trash everything, but I could still tell my stuff was out of place. My space had been invaded and I'd spent hours righting things and scrubbing anything I thought they may have touched. I could still feel their presence in the house, and it really bothered me. With time, I suspected that would fade.

As I meandered through the big farmhouse while drinking my coffee the next morning, I decided that after the murder had been solved, I'd start some renovations and truly make it mine. Tommy had preferred neutral colors, or "man colors," as I liked to call them, and I'd acquiesced. A lot of different shades of brown and beige made up the décor in my home. I wanted a bit more color, which would be easy to achieve without a whole bunch of work. New pillows for the sofa. If I painted one wall in the living room, it would really brighten the space up. I could paint the television stand. I made a mental note to go to the hardware store and get some color samples.

Yes, it was definitely time to put Tommy in my past and make my house my own.

I pulled out my cell phone and dialed him.

"Tilly? What's up?"

"Come get your stuff," I said without preamble. "I'm holding it until next Friday, then I'm donating it."

"Why would you do that?"

"Because I'm putting my relationship with you behind me. You're a no good, cheating pig and I'm done with you."

"Tilly, that's not very nice. I've got a kid! I'm busy with—"

"I don't care, Tommy. Pick it up by next Friday or you can go buy it back from Goodwill over in Cedarville."

A small smile tugged at my lips as I hung up. It felt good to finally be putting him behind me. I wouldn't wallow in what could have been or what I thought we should have had together. He'd shown his true colors, and I didn't want any part of it.

I would also change my last name.

When Tommy had left, I'd been so devastated, my life, my hopes and dreams all disintegrated around me, leaving me with barely enough energy to get out of bed in the morning. Things were different now, and if I was going to cut Tommy out of my life, that meant getting rid of his last name. I'd go back to my maiden name: Bordeaux. With cleaning out his stuff and dropping his name, I'd effectively erase him from my life.

He called me back, but I didn't answer. Instead, I placed the phone on the counter and hurried upstairs to shower. On a whim, I stepped on the scale and screamed in delight at the five pounds I'd lost. Tinker and Belle trotted in to see what all my noise was about. I jumped around and clapped while Tinker barked and Belle left for quieter corners. Not only was I putting Tommy behind me, but also the weight I'd gained because of the breakup. I was shedding my past both literally and figuratively. Things were truly looking up for me.

After my shower, I grabbed my keys and went outside. Tinker ran around the house to greet me and I waved when I saw Mr. Rupert working on the fence close to my property. I went over to say hello.

"How's it going, Mr. Rupert?"

"Just checking the fence," he said, holding up a nail. "Minnie's cows like to lean on it and break it, so I'm shoring it up."

"They're like the Houdini of the animal kingdom," I said. "It's like they have opposable thumbs and can work the locks."

He grinned and nodded. "You're right. Of course, it would help if their owner were a little more responsible with them."

I really didn't want to get into Minnie and her cows. They were her babies, and none of us would probably ever understand.

"What are you going to do with the orchard?" I asked. I stared over his shoulder at the Forest of Evil.

"They're actually coming next week to begin bulldozing this back area," he said.

"Are you going to replant?"

"I'm not sure. It's a lot of work. Sharon and I aren't getting any younger. We're still evaluating the finances to see if we can make it."

"That's too bad," I said, truly disappointed. "The trees were so pretty, especially when they were in bloom. From upstairs in my house, it was like a sea of pink. I really liked looking at them."

Mr. Rupert hitched a thumb over his shoulder. "Well, maybe we'll plant a few. I don't know. Even bare land would be better than having this mess as a view, right?"

"Yes, you're right."

"Where you off to, Tilly?"

I told him about my ideas for making the house my own and he nodded approvingly. "I was really glad when you didn't move when Tommy left. We don't see you or talk to you much, but you're a good neighbor, good people."

"Thank you." A blush crept into my cheeks. "Likewise."

"I better get back to my fence. Good luck with the paint samples."

With a wave, I headed back to my truck. As Tinker bounded toward me from the chicken coop, I asked her if she wanted to take a ride into town. She was more than happy to accompany me and leapt in the truck.

We rode into town together with the windows down, the summer breeze blowing through our hair. I didn't bother with the radio, preferring the sound of the wind racing through the cab instead.

I fully expected to get more nasty looks while I searched for my perfect paint colors, and that was okay. Betty Frank had threatened Mr. York. There wasn't any doubt about that. Whether she meant it as karma coming for him or sticking a knife in his chest, that remained to be seen. The sheriff would most certainly go to the other people on the list of suspects I'd given him and tell them he'd gotten their names from me. People were going to be angry with me, call me a snitch and a whole list of other names, but I could handle it. If it helped find the killer, then great. Someone had tried to frame me by planting the knife in my house and making an anonymous call to the police. At least I hadn't tried to hide my accusations. Whoever the killer was didn't care if an innocent person went to jail, and to me, that meant they'd stop at nothing to be certain they didn't get caught.

Townspeople would also have heard about the Sheriff searching my house based on an anonymous tip. They'd wonder if I was the killer and if I was doing exactly what Connor had accused me of—casting blame on others so I wasn't suspected. I had nothing to hide, so they could believe what they wanted. I tried not to worry and think of the thousands of people who were serving time for a crime they didn't commit.

The situation was very disturbing, but I wouldn't let it disrupt my good mood. I had every intention of finding the killer and proving my innocence. I wasn't sure how I'd go about doing that, but I would. The sheriff could bet his Stetson on that one. Before, solving the murder had been more of a guessing game, but it had become imperative to save my own hide.

And, if I solved the murder, I'd also discover who lit the fireworks and why. Unless Mr. York had been out of his mind before he died like Debbie had suggested.

My phone vibrated in the seat between Tilly and me, but I ignored it. I figured it would be Tommy again, and he was part of my past. I needed to focus on the future and listening to him complain about how busy he had become with his new family wouldn't add to my happiness. I'd told him to get his stuff and I meant it.

My lucky day. A parking spot right in front of the hardware store during the weekend.

"Stay here, Tinker," I said, giving her chin a scratch. "I won't be too long."

I walked into the store with my head held high.

A few stares bore into my back but ignoring them came easy.

As I carefully studied the paint chips, I couldn't decide on colors. At first I thought a light blue would look really nice in the living room, but the yellow would sure brighten it up, although maybe too much. I didn't want to be blinded when the afternoon sun came blazing through the windows, especially in the summer.

I finally compromised and decided to buy a pint of both. I'd paint the wall half yellow and half blue, and see which one I liked the best.

The phone vibrated in my pocket as I paid, but once again I decided not to answer.

Tinker greeted me with a tail wag when I emerged from the store. I placed the paint in the truck bed and we were off.

"Are you excited about painting?" I asked her. "I sure am. I can't wait to add some color to the living room."

My phone rang again and I slipped it out of my pocket. "Yes?"

"Have you gotten that insurance thing taken care of?" Tommy asked. "If you're going to get rid of my stuff, I don't want to be paying for your insurance anymore."

"Yes, I called. You can cancel the policy. I'm just waiting for some papers."

Silence stretched from the other end, and for a moment I thought he'd hung up.

"Are you really taking my stuff to Goodwill? That's pretty cold."

I sighed and pulled off the road. "Tommy, you and I are done. What's cold is cheating on your wife. You've moved on with your life, so let me do the same. Yes. If you don't come get your stuff by Friday, it's going to Goodwill."

"Sometimes I miss you," he whispered. "Sometimes, I want to come back to you."

I gasped in surprise while my heart skipped a couple of beats. For a brief second, pure joy surged through me, but then a profound sadness drowned it out. I could never trust him again, even if I wanted to.

"Tommy, you live your life with your new wife and your kids. I wish you well."

Tears sprung to my eyes as I put the truck in gear again. I reached over and pet Tinker who then laid her head on my lap.

"I'm not going to let him get me down," I muttered.

By the time I arrived home, I had been able

shake a bit of the melancholy. I stopped at my mailbox and pulled out a stack of mail three inches high. I really needed to check it more often.

When we parked in front of the house, Tinker took off to the chicken coop. I stuffed the mail under my arm and grabbed my two cans of paint, then gently set them by the front door. After dumping the mail on the kitchen table, I retrieved a glass of water, then sat down to go through the stack.

"Bills, bills, bills," I mumbled, quickly glancing at the envelopes and deciding what was junk. The insurance paperwork had come, and I ripped it open.

Except it wasn't paperwork. It was a check. A *huge* check.

My heart thundered as I turned over the envelope. It belonged to the insurance company I had settled on, but it wasn't addressed to me.

The new mail sorter had struck again.

I set down the check and stared at it for a good long while, my brain churning. I had no idea how long I sat at the kitchen table, but I had been concentrating so hard, I actually screamed and startled when Belle jumped up and sat down in front of me.

"You scared me, Belly-Belle," I whispered, stroking her head.

When I'd calmed down, I dialed Debbie.

"What's up, Tilly?"

"I need you and Carla to come over here."

"Sure! Should I bring donuts?"

"No. I just figured out who killed Mr. York and I need your help."

21

"ARE YOU POSITIVE?" Carla asked as we sat around my kitchen table, the stress hanging over us like a wet blanket.

"Yes. It's the only thing that makes sense. Like Debbie said, all the pieces fit perfectly, and we know who murdered Mr. York and set off the fireworks."

"So now what?" Debbie asked.

"Now, we head over there and confront him."

"Are you sure you don't want to call the sheriff?" Carla asked.

"No. Not after the way he's treated me. And then the killer will know I'm on to him. What if the sheriff doesn't make an arrest right away? I'm a sitting duck. I'll go to him once I have the proof."

They exchanged nervous glances.

"He's not going to hurt anyone if there's three of us there," I said. "We can overpower him easily."

"I should have brought Big Bertha," Debbie mumbled.

"We don't need her," I said firmly. "We just need a confession."

"Okay, let's go," Carla said with a sigh.

We stood and marched out the front door and across my property. When we got to the fence line, I took a deep breath and slid through the slats. My foot caught on the bottom one and I ended up sprawled across the scorched earth.

"Come on, Grace," Debbie said, grabbing my elbow and hauling me to my feet. If we hadn't been so nervous, we would have laughed until we cried.

"Just one second," I said. "I want to look at something."

I hurried over to the fence that separated the Ruperts' from Minnie's house and pulled on the top slat. It gave way with little effort, and a nail fell to the ground. I suspected as much.

We walked through the burnt orchard and stopped where their backyard began for a moment. Were they home? Maybe I should call the sheriff, or at least Byron. But I knew in my bones they wouldn't listen to me unless I had absolute proof.

I glanced over at Minnie's place and noted Sunflower and Tulip staring at us, then I recalled what Minnie had said. *I can't help it if they like nectarines!*

Bill Rupert opened the back door and waved as we crossed the lawn.

"What can I do for you ladies?"

"We wanted to talk to you, if that's okay," I replied.

"Of course. Come in."

We hung a right and walked into the kitchen. The blue and red chicken theme reminded me of the blue and red hilt of the knife he'd hidden in my house. Any uncertainty I had before vanished.

After I made the introductions, we all sat down at the kitchen table.

I took a deep breath and eyed the killer.

"You killed Mr. York, and it was you who lit the fireworks."

Mr. Rupert's eyes widened and his cheeks reddened. "What the heck, Tilly?"

"Here's your insurance check for the orchard damage," I said, pulling it out of my pocket. "When I interviewed you for the paper, you said you were going to be fine, financially. You weren't lying, were you?"

He stared at the check for a moment, then glanced around the table. "Where did you get this?"

"It was in my mail and I accidentally opened it. I was waiting for papers from the same company."

He picked up the check and studied it again. "This doesn't mean that I killed anyone. It means the insurance company came through quickly for my loss."

I shook my head. "Betty Frank was on the secret committee to bring back the Fourth of July. Sharon told me she was one of her best friends and had been for years. Friends talk, so she told Sharon about Mr. York keeping the fireworks. You overheard them and you figured out a perfect way to destroy the land because Minnie's cows weren't doing it fast enough, even though you kept loosening the fence so they'd barge in here and eat the fruit."

"You're out of your mind," he whispered. "You've gone completely bonkers."

"I don't think so," I replied. "The fireworks were a perfect way for you to burn down the orchard. I think Mr. York saw you do it and he confronted you the next morning. Why he didn't just tell the police that night, I don't know. My guess is that you went over there to make sure he hadn't seen you, or something like that. Or you wanted to know what he told the police. He said he was going to turn you in, and you stabbed him."

Bill threw his head back and laughed. "This is unbelievable. You should be a writer. No one could make up a story like this!"

I ignored him and continued on. "Except, you didn't kill Mr. York like you thought. I found him and he told me whoever lit the fireworks had also stabbed him. And then do you know what he did when I asked who it was?"

He shook his head.

"Mr. York pointed to the sky. I thought he meant the birds, God, a cloud... I had no idea. But now I'm certain he was pointing up. R-*U*-*P*-E-R-T. Your darn name. He told me right then and there who did it but I didn't understand."

I stood and began pacing the kitchen. I'd given a lot of thought to my theory, and it made perfect sense. All the pieces fit. But actually saying it out loud... well, I'd never been more certain I was right about anything in my life. I glanced over at Debbie and Carla, who nodded, encouraging me to continue.

"You most likely heard through the town gossip that I had a list of suspects."

"He did know," Debbie said. "He came in for

coffee one morning, and I was talking to someone. He heard about Derek's money and your theory on the mayor."

"In this whole mess, I looked at you as the victim," I said, placing my hands on the back of the chair I had been sitting in. "It never occurred to me that the victim could be the instigator. Maybe you thought I was getting too close, even though I never suspected you. Maybe you were just worried. You had to give the police someone on a silver platter, but I couldn't figure out why me."

Bill crossed his arms over his chest and shook his head.

"You planted that knife in Tilly's place," Carla spat. "How dare you try to frame my friend?"

"How would I have gotten in her house?" Bill asked. "What am I? A genie? You ladies need to start using your brains."

"I actually thought about that," I said. "Remember when we first moved in and you and Sharon came over to welcome us? I had locked myself out of the house and you saw where I grabbed the spare key. We never moved it, which was dumb. But then again, I never thought my neighbor would commit murder."

"Tilly, I appreciate you coming over and sharing

this crazy theory with me, as well as bringing me my mail, but I think you need to leave now. This is ridiculous, and I'm beginning to wonder if you've been spending too much time with the York boy and your brains are fried on drugs."

"I don't do drugs, Mr. Rupert," I said through clenched teeth. "It's outright rude for you to say that."

"Okay, then," he said, holding his hands out to the sides. "I'm sorry, but I didn't light those fireworks and I didn't kill Henry York. I don't know what else to tell you."

He seemed so sure of himself and self-doubt began to creep in. Had I been wrong?

No. The Ruperts' had benefitted from the fire. If I hadn't found that big, fat check, I never would have suspected them. Everything fit together, not like the other suspects on my list. With them, one piece of the puzzle had been missing, but not with the Ruperts.

"You had motive," I said. "You told me the orchard was getting to be too much to handle. You burnt it to the ground with the fireworks. Mr. York knew it, so you killed him. You walk away with the check. It was you, Bill. Quit lying."

"Go to the police," he said as he slowly stood.

"Go and tell them your crazy theory. They're just going to laugh at you again."

I pursed my lips together. How did I make him confess? I needed *proof* of what he'd done. Rushing over to the kitchen drawers, I quickly pulled them open. I could immediately see that they were far more organized than mine, and I hoped that boded well for my search.

"Hey!" Bill yelled above the clacking of utensils sliding around. "Get out of there! What the heck is wrong with you?"

I found it on my last drawer. The knife was the exact replica of the one I'd discovered in my house and the one I'd seen planted in Mr. York's chest.

With a grin, I turned around slowly while holding it up in front of me. "This is it, Bill. Here's the proof I need. Admit what you did."

"He didn't do it," Sharon said, coming around the corner. I hadn't even realized she was home. "I did it. Everything you said is true, except Bill didn't kill Henry York. Henry didn't tell the police I was responsible because he wanted me to be accountable for what I'd done and turn myself in."

I exchanged confused glances with Carla and Debbie. Stabbing someone was an intimate crime, so we'd suspected a man of having done it. Historically, women tended to be much sneakier and kill with poisons.

"Sharon," Bill said, rushing to her side. "Why? Why would you do such a thing?"

"For that," she replied, pointing at the check on the table. "I've always hated that damned orchard. It's so much work and so little financial reward... I told you I wanted out. I told you I didn't want any part of it, but you didn't listen, Bill. I had to take matters into my own hands."

When I'd interviewed them, Sharon had been so upset, I'd thought it was from the loss of her orchard, but I'd obviously been wrong. Maybe despondent over killing Mr. York, but definitely not sad about the trees.

"We were talking about how to best get out from under it, Sharon," Bill said, placing his hands on her shoulders.

"No, we weren't. I was talking and you were telling me we'd discuss it some other time. I'm tired, Bill. I want to retire. I want to travel. With the orchard, we're never going to make money, let alone break even. It had to go."

"Why didn't you just sell the place?" Carla asked.

"I offered that as an option, but he wouldn't listen," Sharon said, tears running down her cheeks.

"Typical man," Debbie mumbled.

"I didn't want to start the fire or kill York. I tried to get Minnie's cows to destroy it. They loved the nectarines. Therefore, I loosened up the fencing whenever I got the chance so they'd barge onto our property. But they weren't demolishing it fast enough."

"Sharon, I almost killed them," Bill said incredulously. "I was this close to shooting them. And all the things I said to Minnie? And you were responsible for it?"

"It doesn't matter now," Sharon said, wiping her face. "We've got the insurance check. We can do whatever we want."

"I don't even know you anymore," Bill whispered, shaking his head. "How could you do this?"

"Um, there's three of us in here who don't think you'll be doing much of anything," Debbie said, getting to her feet. "You tried to frame Tilly for the murder you committed, and frankly, that doesn't sit well with us."

"You killed your neighbor!" I yelled. "Do you really think you're going to get away with that?"

"Go to the police then," Sharon said, her voice calm, even, and a special kind of crazy. "Go and tell them your theory on how the upstanding, lifelong citizen of Oak Peak, Sharon Rupert, killed her neighbor. Everyone already thinks you're bonkers, Tilly, because of the list of suspects you gave to the sheriff. I can't believe you accused Betty Frank of such a thing. The man is just going to look at you like you're insane again."

"You put that knife in my house?" I asked, closing the space between us. "You wanted me to go down for a murder you committed?"

"Why not? You had your nose up in everyone's business writing your articles for the paper. Why not you?"

I shook my head as I gripped the hilt. "You shouldn't have done that, Sharon."

She simply stared at me and I grew more furious by the second. My hands began to shake and the angry heat singed my cheeks.

"Prove it," she whispered. "Go to the police. You're Crazy Tilly Donner and no one is going to believe you."

"It's Bordeaux. Tilly Bordeaux," I said through gritted teeth. "And, I don't think they'll have any trouble believing me when they hear three recordings of this conversation."

I slipped my phone out of my pocket, as did Debbie and Carla.

Sharon stared at all of us. When she realized what we'd done, her eyes widened in fear and fury. Her hands fisted at her sides. Then, she let out a cry that shook me to my bones. With the pain and anger emanating from it, I almost felt sorry for her.

Almost.

EPILOGUE

Fourth of July

"THANK YOU," I said to Mrs. Bonner as she scooped another helping of barbecue beef onto my plate. "This is certainly delicious."

And I really looked forward to chowing it down, as well as the sugar free chocolate cake on my other plate given to me by Debbie, of course.

The police had completed their investigation into the fireworks and Mr. York's murder. With our recordings, a warrant for the Rupert house, and some blood samples, they'd come to the conclusion that Sharon York had been guilty of both crimes.

Duh.

Life had returned to normal. My boss, Harold,

complained that nothing happened in this area, but at the same time, he left his truck running while he picked up toner at the office supply store. I'd ended up painting my living room blue. The yellow had been blinding in the summer sun, and the blue reminded me of happiness, bright skies, and the ocean. I was really thrilled with the final product, especially since I'd also painted the credenza and TV stand white. One of the upstairs bedrooms had been turned into my office and Tommy had never come for his stuff, so I gave it to Goodwill. I may have cried a tear or two over that, but I held my ground.

I'd dug up the knife Sharon planted in my house and given it to the sheriff. He'd been furious with me but understood why I'd hidden it.

I didn't like the chickens any more than before, but I couldn't get rid of them and break Tinker's heart. She loved spending time with them out by the coop.

I began to expand my writing and started doing some freelance work for some magazines. I even started a mystery novel. That wasn't going so well, but I was writing, and Harold always told me that's what writers did: they'd write. He said one can't edit a blank page, so I continued to plug away at it. One day, I hoped to see my work displayed at the bookstore.

After all the hoopla over the fireworks going off, the mayor had opened up a town meeting to discuss bringing back the holiday to Oak Peak. No more secret committees—everyone had a say. A lot of discussion and fighting ensued, but it had been agreed upon that the town would celebrate the holiday, albeit without fireworks. People warmed to the idea of a town potluck and some businesses on Oak Avenue actually decorated to commemorate the holiday. Even though City Hall now sat where the original tragic celebration had taken place, it did have a huge grassy area that surrounded the building, and that was where the mayor had decided to hold the festivities. Tables were laid out for people to set out their food, Mayor Shelton gave a rousing speech after a few too many beers, and everyone seemed to enjoy themselves.

And some of those people could really cook!

I joined Debbie, Carla and her husband, Mac, on a blanket. The sun had disappeared behind the mountain and the temperature had begun to drop. Some kids ran around with sparklers while everyone else gorged on the delicious food.

It was nice to be part of a community event. I

waved and smiled at a few people I knew, and even Betty Frank gave me a small nod of greeting, although the hatchet hadn't been completely buried. I'd sent her best friend to prison.

After Sharon Rupert was taken to jail, Bill Rupert disappeared. No one knew where he'd gone, but Minnie's cows freely roamed the orchard and ate the remaining fruit off the trees.

The fire department came to the conclusion that the mayor had purchased off-brand, illegal fireworks, which was why they'd sparked the blaze in the orchard with such ease. Usually, fireworks used in community celebrations burnt out before they hit the ground. With Sharon lighting the whole darn shed on fire, the orchard didn't stand a chance. The mayor apologized to the town and paid a fine, but that was the end of it. We would see if the people of Oak Peak remembered the event come election time.

Debbie had released her sugar-free line of pastries and everyone loved them. She was receiving requests for pies and cakes. I didn't see much of her unless I went into her store because she devoted every waking hour to perfecting her recipes or baking her special orders. She needed to hire someone to help her, but she waved off my suggestion.

I glanced over at Carla and Mac as they kissed each other. They were obviously terribly in love, and it brought me joy to see her so happy.

With a sigh, I finished the last of my barbecue sandwich. I'd lost a total of ten pounds, and I began to berate myself for overeating, but then decided to just enjoy it and get back on track tomorrow.

I'd barely seen Derek. He came over after Sharon was arrested and thanked me for solving his dad's murder, but then he left town and I had no idea where he'd gone or if he was coming back. I kept an eye on his place and found myself disappointed every morning when I didn't see his SUV there.

After a while, people began packing up their blankets and food to head home. Mac and Carla left and Debbie stretched out.

"I'm exhausted," she said as she shut her eyes.

"You need help at the bakery. I keep telling you that."

"I know, I know. Do you know how hard it is to find good help these days?"

"You haven't even looked," I replied, rolling my eyes. "Try throwing an ad in the paper before you start complaining."

"Hey, Tilly."

I glanced over my shoulder to find Derek

standing behind me. My heart fluttered as I scrambled to my feet. "Hi! Where have you been?"

He chuckled and I noted his eyes were green in the twilight. "Do you want to walk with me for a bit?"

"Sure. I'll be right back, Debbie."

She waved but didn't open her eyes. I wouldn't be surprised if I came back to find her asleep.

"You look pretty tonight," he said with a grin.

I quickly looked away and ran my hand down the front of my pink T-shirt. "Thank you."

Mama always said pink was my color.

My stomach churned with nerves as we wandered around the dispersing party. "So, where have you been?"

"I had to go pack up the rest of my stuff and finish some business."

"Does that mean you're staying for good? You're going to be making your dad's house your own?"

"It sure does."

I liked Derek and having him as a neighbor made me happy. I smiled up at him as we stopped and faced each other.

"I was wondering something about you," he said.

"What's that?"

Gosh, he was cute. What had Carla said? Cute as

a bunny butt. That most certainly described him. In a manly way, of course.

Derek wiped his hands down the front of his jeans. Was it nerves or the heat? I found the summer night quite nice.

"I was wondering if maybe you'd go out to dinner with me sometime."

Oh, my word.

Derek wanted to take me out? On a date? Or out as in a neighbor asking another neighbor to have dinner?

Was I ready to date again? What if I did go and I ended up not liking him, like I had with Byron? Could I live with disliking my neighbor? Things would be weird between us, wouldn't they?

I had been feeling pretty good about myself lately, but the thought of *dating* Derek scared the heck out of me. Maybe a meal with a neighbor would be better?

Sweat formed on my brow and my heart thundered. The pleasant night air suddenly became incredibly warm. I had no idea how to answer.

"What do you think, Tilly?" he asked. "Will you go out with me?"

ABOUT THE AUTHOR

Carly Winter is the pen name for a USA Today best-selling and award-winning romance author.

When not writing, she enjoys spending time with her family, reading and enjoying the fantastic Arizona weather (except summer - she doesn't like summer). She does like dogs, wine and chocolate and wishes Christmas happened twice a year.

CarlyWinterCozyMysteries.com

CPSIA information can be obtained
at www.ICGtesting.com
Printed in the USA
LVHW091146121222
735043LV00031B/1329

9 781732 123687